USA *TODAY* BESTSELLING AUTHOR
DALE MAYER

Jewels in .the Juniper

Lovely Lethal Gardens 10

JEWELS IN THE JUNIPER: LOVELY LETHAL GARDENS, BOOK 10
Beverly Dale Mayer
Valley Publishing Ltd.

Copyright © 2020

ISBN-13: 978-1-773362-71-7
Print Edition

Books in This Series:

Boxed Sets and Bundles
https://geni.us/Bundlepage

About This Book

A new cozy mystery series from *USA Today* best-selling author Dale Mayer. Follow gardener and amateur sleuth Doreen Montgomery—and her amusing and mostly lovable cat, dog, and parrot—as they catch murderers and solve crimes in lovely Kelowna, British Columbia.

Riches to rags. ... Chaos is still present ... Memories are fading ... but not for everyone...!

The problem with notoriety is unfair expectations. When Mack's mother, Millicent requests Doreen's help with a problem she's kept hidden for decades, Doreen feels obligated to help. What harm could it do? Except maybe piss Mack off. Something she did on a regular basis anyway.

Considering it involves a small bag of jewels, a failed marriage, a jewelry store burned decades ago, possible insurance fraud and maybe... murder...

With her trusty trio of furry and feathered cohorts, she's brings an old case to today's issue and finds it's more current than ever...

Sign up to be notified of all Dale's releases here!

https://geni.us/DaleNews

Prologue

Friday Morning …

I T HAD BEEN two days since Doreen had been at Ed
Burns's house. She'd kept her head low and had stayed
out of sight since then. It was Friday morning, and she was
back at Millicent's place. Millicent hadn't stopped talking
since Doreen had arrived to weed, but that was okay. Doreen
was more than happy to listen while Millicent reminisced
about the Jude and Ed Burns family drama and then about
Frank and Fred Darbunkle.

"You, my dear, are an absolute marvel," Millicent said.

"Not at all," Doreen said. "Who knew I would find out
all this just from finding one ice pick in the ivy?"

Millicent chuckled. "Did I ever tell you about the jewels
I found?"

Doreen sat back on her haunches. "Jewels? Where?"

"They were in the juniper," Millicent said. "It was years
and years ago. I never did find out who they belonged to."

"Did you ask Mack to find out?"

"Mack wasn't even an officer back then. Not sure I have
mentioned them to him since he joined law enforcement,
now that I think about it." She frowned. "You know what?

I'll see if I can find them."

"Especially if you want to find who they belong to," Doreen said. "It might take time to find the owners."

Millicent looked at Doreen and smiled. "Not with you, my dear. You are so darn fast. I'll take a look now because I want you to have the jewels, and I want you to find out who they belong to."

"Oh, but …" Doreen started.

However, it was too late. Millicent was gone.

Doreen laughed. Apparently she now had a new cold case.

Chapter 1

Friday Late Morning ...

D OREEN WALKED HOME slowly, her three animals at her side. She had just left a very rattled Millicent, who couldn't find the jewels she had been talking about. Doreen didn't know whether Mack's mother was serious about her story or if her memory was starting to go and maybe she was imagining it all. Doreen hoped not because it sounded like a fun new mystery and likely to be something completely harmless. She was getting tired of being attacked on these jobs. On the other hand, Mack wouldn't like it if his mother was involved in one of Doreen's cases.

As Doreen and her animals hit the creek, she turned to see Goliath dragging behind. She crouched and called him to her. He stretched, looking toward her. She smiled as she reached an arm around him, picked up the big orange Maine coon cat, and continued along the path on the creek's edge. Goliath was perfectly content to be carried. Only then Thaddaeus wanted up too.

With Thaddeus secured on her shoulder, he stared at Goliath, clearly unimpressed at having to share some of Doreen's love and attention. She reached up a hand and patted Thaddeus too. "You're fine, Thaddeus."

He crooned in her ear, gently rubbing his head against hers. Then Goliath reached up and nudged her with his head, which was his way of mimicking that he loved her too.

Mugs took note of that but was clearly assured of her love for him as he seemed to smile at them. She chuckled and, with her hefty armload, continued toward her place. The river was higher than it had been, but she wasn't up on the details of the fluctuations in water levels. She knew sometimes it rose with the water coming down off the mountains—with the highest levels in the wee hours of the morning—then receded and sometimes rose again, depending on the temperature and the snowmelt. But now it was definitely higher, and the sound of the river babbling beside her was lovely.

Although named Mission Creek, it was river-sized, and no way would she try to cross it right now. With the water's force and flow, she doubted she'd make it without being swept out to the lake.

And that thought reminded her of another case she'd previously worked on, where a little boy and a handyman had gone missing. She was grateful she'd managed to find their bodies in the lake and to bring the families closure.

She didn't want to think about the ice pick scenario she had just dealt with. She wanted to enjoy days of gardening and visiting her grandmother and maybe finding a secondhand bookstore to take the place of the library, so she didn't come under the gimlet eye of the librarian on the night shift again. Back home, she lowered Goliath to the ground as soon as she came around the corner. "You can walk the rest of the way, pudge."

Mugs barked at Goliath, then ran a short way forward

before slowing down, dropping his big nose on the path and sniffing.

She stopped and spied some new boards stacked on the ground by her house. She frowned and headed around the side of the house closest to her neighbor, Richard de Genaro. Everything was still here—all the big cinder blocks and the beams she and Mack had stacked there—but now a bunch of two-by-fours had been added.

As she carried on to the front of the house, she heard another big clattering noise. It was Arnold, the older cop Doreen had met on her first day here, delivering the two-by-fours. "Hey, Arnold. You got those to spare?"

"Sure do. My wife has been on me about cleaning out that shed," he said. "I don't know how many of these at this length you can use, but Mack said to bring it all, and he'd take care of getting rid of what you don't need afterward." He grinned at her. "Best deal yet. I can save myself ten bucks not taking it to the dump."

"Right," Doreen said, as she looked at the wood. "And hopefully we'll have a use for them all."

Then he brought out two very long and fat boards.

"Wow, what are those for?"

"They're perfect for stair stringers," he said, "depending on how many steps you'll cut in."

She nodded as if she knew what that meant, though it made no sense to her. Why would you have *string* and *stair* in the same sentence? Surely steps should be made from something solid. But then, as she studied the boards, they looked like they were pretty solid, at one and a half or maybe two inches thick. And they were really long. She didn't know what length for sure. Still, she was happy to have them. "Do you know how long they are?"

"They're about four and a half feet each," he said, "and I've got four of them."

"What were you doing with them?"

"I was supposed to put steps off the deck, but then my wife changed her mind and wanted railing all around the top."

Then Doreen understood. "Got it. That's what these are for, the steps off my deck."

"It will cost you a little bit more money," he said, "but, if you can get some more spare pieces, you'll be doing fine."

"I sure hope so," she said. "I'm still trying to figure out what to put on the surface."

"Well, if you get that forever stuff, you won't have to maintain it or repaint every ten years. But wood decking is much nicer. We put wood on, then figure we can paint it once. After that it'll be somebody else's problem," Arnold said with a hoarse laugh.

She smiled. "I think wood is just fine for now." She didn't know why he'd bring her bad wood though. The beams were, … well, … green. Were they supposed to be?

"And, of course, we pretty much used up all the railings we had," he said. "I might have a few of the metal rails but not likely too many."

"I can talk to Mack and see what he thinks."

As Arnold dropped the last beam on the ground, he said, "Tell you what. I'll talk to him when I go back to the office next."

"You're not working today?"

"Nope. I took the day off. The wife's planning on having the family come around this weekend," he said with a grimace. "Wanted me to clean up all this stuff first."

Doreen grinned at that. "Don't you just love honey-do

lists?"

He glared at her. "Nope, I don't." And, with that, he walked to the end of his truck and snapped his tailgate closed, then gave her a partial wave and hopped into his truck and drove off.

Delighted, Doreen raced back around to the stack of supplies; it was so much bigger. Not only that but boards she hadn't seen delivered lay stacked in front of her. Someone else's contribution. She pulled out her phone and started talking the moment Mack answered. "Arnold was just here, delivering stair stringers and some two-by-fours."

"Perfect," he said. "How does the wood look?"

She hesitated. "Like wood? Only green. I don't understand why you would bring in bad wood."

"Bad wood?"

"It's green," she said, as if that should have been explanation enough. He sputtered with laughter at the other end of the phone. She glared at it. "You're doing it again," she warned.

"What?" he asked between the chuckles.

"You're laughing at me."

"Laughing *with* you," he said.

"Except I don't seem to be laughing, nor do I see anything funny to be laughing about." She glared around her, looking for other green wood.

"The green means it's treated," he said.

"Treated how?" she asked, and a phrase popped out of her mouth. "With respect?"

At that, he started off again with great big guffaws of laughter. "No. Treated so it won't rot."

"Oh," she said, her voice lowered to a sigh. Of course they didn't want the wood to rot. But then why weren't the two-by-fours treated too?

"Besides," he said, "once it's all in place, those stringers will be hard to see because they'll have steps on top of them."

She studied the boards and nodded, though in complete confusion. "Good." Then she strengthened the tone of her voice. "As long as you know what you're doing. Will it be a green deck?"

"We can get treated boards in brown too," he said. "It all depends on what you want to do. We can put decking boards on top, and they'll look like natural wood. You'll have to stain it with Varathane or put some other preservative coating on it. Or we can get boards already treated that look more natural."

"More natural would be nice," she said.

"We're not there yet."

"No, but we're getting a lot of lumber," she said in surprise. "Arnold brought four of those stringer boards."

"That's great," Mack said, "because that will do two complete sets of steps or a heck of a long one."

"You need two for a set of steps?"

"Imagine that we'll notch out triangles on each of the boards and rest steps on them," he explained. "So you need two per set. But, if we'll do one all down the long side of the deck, we'll have to space those stringers every three feet across, or maybe four, and then you can put long boards all the way across the steps."

She nodded, but she didn't have a clue what he meant about notching triangles. Still, she figured she'd given him enough to laugh at for the day. "So what else do we need?"

"Decking boards," he said, "and railings, then the hardware to put it all together."

"Right," she said, "and the railings are pretty expensive,

aren't they?"

"They are," he said, "which is another reason to consider just doing steps all the way around."

She walked around where the deck would be built. "Particularly if we already have four stringers."

"Not sure that'll be enough yet," he warned.

"Okay," she said. "Whenever you get a chance, you can always come by, take a look, and see what else we might need."

"I was talking to one of the guys here. He's got a bunch of anchors and some of the hardware. He finished his deck, and he's still got a lot of screws, so I was hoping to snag leftovers from him too."

She smiled in delight. "Wow, this is quite a process you've got going here."

"Everybody has leftovers after these projects," he said. "The trick is making sure you get enough of what you need and don't end up taking too much of the stuff you won't need."

"Right, but, if the decking boards are all different kinds and colors, chances are we won't get enough of one kind to do the whole deck, will we?"

"Not likely," he said cheerfully. "It's a matter of seeing if we can find any, and, if we can't, that becomes the cost you'll bear."

"Right," she said, wincing at the loud *cha-ching* in her mind.

"But, after we gather up all these leftovers, I'm pretty sure we can get a quote for close to one thousand to top off what you need."

At that, she brightened. "Seriously?"

"Yep," he said. "I'll stop by and have a look but not today." His words came on a heavy sigh. "We're a little busy with paperwork and interviewing various people."

"Sorry about all the extra work," she said in a cheery voice. "I get to walk away now, whereas you don't."

"Isn't that the truth." His words were a half growl. "On the other hand, we can hardly be too upset when you're helping us close all these cases."

"You know that it does make me wonder just what you guys have been doing for the last decade or two." Her words were delivered in a bland tone. "Considering I just arrived and the number of cases we've closed ..."

"Hardly sitting on our butts," he said. "Believe me. Plenty of jokes have come our way about the lack of police effort on some of these cases. And it's hardly fair, with you working one case at a time, while we have tons of active cases."

She winced at that. "You're right. It isn't fair, and I know I'm not doing anything you guys wouldn't do, if you had the spare man-hours."

"If we had spare man-hours," he repeated, "we could do all kinds of stuff."

She could hear the fatigue and the frustration in his voice and knew it wasn't fair for her to egg him on. She was only doing it because he had laughed at her earlier. Then again, she still wanted to ask questions about stringers and decking but didn't think it would work out so well for her. "We were talking about dinner," she said cautiously.

"I can't do it tonight," he said regretfully. "I'll be lucky if I get out of the office today at all."

"You're not sleeping there, are you?"

"It won't be the first time," he said, "although it's typically more like catnaps in my chair. Then I get up and walk around, clearing my head."

"You'd be much better off to go home and to get at least four hours of sleep and then go back refreshed," she said, with just enough of a tone of authority in her voice to make him chuckle.

"What is this?" he asked. "Are you worried about me? And when did you become such an expert on sleepless nights anyway?"

"Well, that was my life," she said. "Not that I was working, but I would sit up and worry."

"Worry about what?"

"My future, my marriage, my lack of children, what I was doing with my life, and how I got into such a loveless marriage, for starters."

"Sorry." A note of surprise was in his voice. "I wasn't expecting to dredge up bad memories."

"No, I'm sure you weren't. I was thinking I do need to talk to your brother, since my second fall through my little bridge canceled our first attempt."

"Good," he said with hearty satisfaction. "I'll set it up."

"Fine," she said, "and it better be soon, otherwise I'll wish I hadn't brought it up."

"Calling him now," Mack said with a chuckle. "I'll let you know how the call goes."

"Good enough," Doreen responded. "I have a few other things I can work on today."

"Work on?"

"Yeah, *work on*," she repeated. "Nothing to do with ice picks or any other cases."

"Good. How about you just work on your garden and leave the rest of this criminal work to us?"

"Sure, as apparently you've got places to go and things to do on your criminal cases," she said with an airy tone of voice, "maybe I will."

Mack snorted at that and hung up.

Doreen grinned and looked down at her phone, realizing just how much she liked talking to him. She placed the phone on the counter, then put on a pot of coffee, and said to her critters, "You know what? It's lunchtime." She was kind of bored and restless, but, at the same time, she was happy. She'd done her day's work at Millicent's, and Mack would owe her money again for the gardening she'd done. Millicent had tantalized Doreen with the thought of another case, but she was happy to put it all off to one side and just rest for a bit.

Maybe a secondhand bookstore would be a good idea. She'd love to grab an armload of books, then come back and chill on her deck. Speaking of her deck, ... maybe she should mark off the accumulated materials from her supply list, so she knew what she would still have to buy. Or maybe it was really just a time to do nothing and to relax. She could visit Nan.

She leaned against the counter as she contemplated her afternoon. It was hard to imagine it could be a bad afternoon when it was a beautiful sunny Friday.

As soon as the coffee was done, she grabbed a cup and walked to her kitchen table, putting down the cup for now because it was too hot to drink. She stared at the papers and files all over the small room and snatched up the basket of newspaper clippings.

Bob Small. She went through the clippings. She hadn't done anything about that serial killer yet. She didn't want to think of it as something that could wait, but it was a big project, and she needed to be at her best to find the clues. And apparently he was suspected of killing over a dozen people, so she didn't want to get into something so horrific without having a fresh notepad and her brain at least turned on. Right now, it felt like her brain sat on the back burner on simmer, humming away, not doing anything useful.

With her cup of coffee in hand, she grabbed her deck supply list, stepped outside, and marked off what she now had for materials versus what she would need. As she studied her list, they didn't have even half the materials yet, but they were a good one-third in. Which meant the cost, as far as she could recalculate, would probably be somewhere around $1,700 now. That was getting a little bit closer to doable.

The decking boards would be pricey; plus she still needed a few more of the big crossbeams. And, of course, the railing was a horrific cost. The steps did alleviate the need for a railing. She would still put a railing down one side of the house for Nan, in case she needed it to get up and down in later years. With that, Doreen walked back inside, tossing the pad of paper on the kitchen table. Then she went back outside, sat down on the edge of the deck, and just stared out at the backyard.

Now that she'd told Mack it was okay to contact his brother for a meeting, she was already wishing she hadn't. It would bring up something she just didn't want to deal with. But she still held so much anger and outrage that her husband, soon to be ex-husband, had treated her as he had. And even more so her own divorce lawyer. Even if Doreen didn't get anything from her husband, which was less important now that she was possibly getting a lot of money from the auction of Nan's antiques, Doreen didn't think her divorce lawyer should get away with doing what she'd done. That wasn't fair. But then, not everybody looked at life the way Doreen did. And it was a little difficult to get people to understand her perspective too.

Still, enough time had gone by that she could look at her marriage, and divorce, a little more objectively and see just what a fool she'd been. She'd been so caught up in her cloistered world that, when it had come time for her husband and her divorce attorney to pull their little shenanigans, Doreen hadn't seen it coming.

Just then Thaddeus walked beside her, hopped onto her knee, and stared up at her, his head tilted.

"What's the matter, buddy?"

He tilted his head to the other side, looked at her again, and then cocked his head the other way.

"Don't you worry about me, sweetie." She smiled, reached out, and gently brushed the feathers on his neck and along his back. "We're doing just fine."

"Thaddeus is here," he said gently. "Thaddeus is here."

Her phone rang, but she didn't recognize the number. "Hello?"

"Doreen, it's Millicent," Mack's mother said. "I found the jewels."

Doreen straightened. "Seriously?"

"Yes," she said, her tone wild with excitement. "Do you want to come and have a look?"

"Do I ever! We're on our way." Doreen reached down and picked up Thaddeus, tucking him up onto her shoulder, and said, "Come on, big guy. Let's go for another walk."

When he heard her say *walk*, Mugs jumped up and down. She put him on the leash just because, and the four of them walked over to Millicent's place. It wasn't that far away, and now she had a reason to be returning, and it wasn't for gardening.

As she walked up to the front door, Millicent opened it

and said, "Come in. Come in."

"You said you never told Mack about this, right?"

"I don't think so, but honestly I don't remember. It's also why I had so much trouble finding where I'd been keeping them all these years."

"Exactly where did you find them?"

"We used to have a big juniper out front." Millicent walked over to the living room window and pointed at the corner of the property between her place and the next property along the road. "A really big one was there. We had this storm one day, and it snapped the top right off and split the trunk. So we cut it off, but then there was this big nasty stump. We left it for a long time. Of course, every once in a while, we dug into the trunk and tried to rot it out, and it finally worked.

"But we still had to work at it to get the rest of it out. It was really bothering my husband, and, one day, when the city guys were around here doing some work with equipment, we asked one of them to just hit the stump a few times with the bucket on his machine, so we could rip it up from the roots. He did as we asked, and, after they were gone, we spent the weekend tearing it apart. And that's when I found this little tiny bag." As she spoke, she held out a very old and faded velvet bag. It was a dark green color.

Doreen reached out a hand for it. "Wow," she said. "This is a jewel bag too, isn't it?"

"That's exactly what I thought," Millicent said, as she led the way into the kitchen. "I did write down a few notes in my journal about it."

She flicked through one of the journals Doreen had seen before.

"Here. I just put *JJ* because I didn't want anybody to

think we had jewels here on the property."

"Of course," Doreen said. "Mack wasn't very old back then, was he?"

"He was just an infant. My husband and I discussed what to do about them, but we just tucked the little bag of jewels away, thinking the right answer would come to us. We had no way to identify whose they were, but we tried, and the police tried. When the jewels weren't claimed in the allotted time frame, the police returned them to us. Yet, at the same time, we didn't really feel we had any right to them, so they ended up just sitting here."

Doreen carefully poured the jewels into her hand. "These are amazing," she marveled. "The gems have been cut beautifully." She picked up one green stone and held it up in the light. It twinkled and flashed with an absolutely glorious color. "Did you ever get them appraised?"

Millicent sat down beside her. "No, we didn't. We felt like something was important about them, but we didn't know how to handle them, so we didn't."

"How do you think Mack will feel after hearing about this now?" Doreen asked.

Millicent wrinkled up her face. "I can handle my boy. He'll be upset. He'll be even more upset that I didn't tell him a long time ago, and I'll just say it never occurred to me. Honestly, I had forgotten all about it until you were talking about your 'ice pick and ivy' thing."

"And then, of course, you thought, 'jewels in the juniper,' and you remembered these."

"Exactly. And, like I said, I now want you to track down who they belong to. They aren't mine. That's for sure."

"And so you just kept them?"

"We figured we'd hold on to them, waiting to find the

true owner. Because we didn't know what else to do."

"You could have sold them," Doreen said gently. She didn't know anything about their financial affairs, but they obviously weren't wealthy, unlike Doreen's soon to be ex-husband. He would have had these appraised and sold in a heartbeat.

"No, it wasn't really our thing," she said. "We knew they weren't ours."

"Never a thought to give them to Mack?"

"Honestly, we put them away and forgot about them," she admitted.

"Good," Doreen said. "I'll get started. Although I'm not sure just where or how."

"I'm giving them to you," Millicent said. "And you can figure out who owned them."

"What if I can't?"

Millicent looked up at her, and Doreen could see the tremble of her lower lip. "It always bothered me, not knowing," she said, "so I hope you can."

"If I can't, I'll give them back to you. How's that?" Doreen said.

Millicent shook her head. She closed the jewels inside Doreen's fingers. "No, you need them. Nobody is giving you anything for all the help you've shown this town. I don't need the jewels. Mack doesn't need the jewels."

"I'm not so sure about that," Doreen said. "They could be worth tens of thousands of dollars."

Millicent's eyebrows raised, and her eyes widened at that. She shook her head. "They're not ours, and that's the bottom line. They're not mine, and I don't feel like I can keep them."

"Let me see what I can do," Doreen repeated, "but you

haven't given me a lot to go on."

"No, I haven't." Millicent stared the jewels, as if mesmerized. "I honestly don't know what to say."

"Do you have a copy of the report that says you handed them over to the police, by any chance?" she asked hopefully.

Millicent looked at her with surprise and then shook her head. "No, I don't. I don't know if Mack might be able to access something like that."

"It was probably too long ago," Doreen said, "unfortunately."

Chapter 2

Friday Afternoon ...

BACK HOME WITH the valuable little bag sitting on her kitchen table, Doreen had good reason to set her security system again. Not that she ever stopped using it because there'd been enough trouble here at home that she hadn't found any sense of peace without it. But it was a makeshift system, a hand-me-down of sorts. Mack would leave it in place until she had enough money to put in a proper one—something she needed to put on her to-do list to handle down the road.

Within minutes of getting home, she had felt her energy draining. She kept staring at the jewels, wondering how she would even begin to find out who owned them. She should have asked Millicent for information on the property, such as how long she'd lived there but, from what Doreen already knew about Millicent and her husband, they had been there for decades. And the juniper tree was clearly already large at the time of its fall, so somebody had either lost the jewels much earlier or had deliberately planted the bag somewhere at the base of the tree. And then, as the tree grew, so did the roots around it, getting bigger and bigger.

On a whim she sat down at her laptop and uploaded an image of the jewelry bag, and then she looked for a match. It was just a green velvet bag. She quickly got a hit on many different jewelry bags. And most had some emblem from the jewelry store. Curious, she picked up hers and carefully put the jewels into a little clear glass bowl, then carried the bag outside into the sun, where she could study the bag better. It was dirty, but maybe, if she cleaned it up, she might find something.

Oh, but there might be DNA on it. At that thought, she couldn't just wash it. She went back inside, grabbed a small tea towel, and gently wiped at the area over her kitchen sink, trying to brush off the dirt that had soaked in. Indeed, something was there, and, with a little brush she used for cleaning the spouts of teapots, she gave the bag a careful bit of a scrub, then added warm water to the brush and lightly brushed the bag again, trying not to remove anything but the dirt. She then took it outside into the sun to dry.

Once that dried a bit, she took a picture of what she could faintly see, then enlarged it. Sure enough, she found the emblem of a jewelry store. Surprised, she sat back. She didn't know why she should be surprised, because, of course, these were jewels and perhaps expensive jewels at that.

So what would make more sense than these gems coming from a jewelry store? She downloaded the image and then tried a reverse lookup, seeking something that would match the emblem. There it was: Johnson and Abelman Jewelers. A quick search revealed it was an old company in Kelowna that had gone bankrupt about thirty-five years ago.

She picked up her phone and placed a call. As soon as Millicent answered, Doreen said, "Millicent, I forgot to ask you for a copy of your journal entries on the jewels while I was there. If there is no police report, your records might help pinpoint the dates regarding finding the jewels and when the police returned them to you." Doreen held on until Millicent returned to the phone with the information asked for.

"We found them April 12, 1982." She sounded winded. "Oh, and I received them back thirty-three days later, on May 15."

"Good enough," Doreen said, writing down the dates. "Have you ever heard of Johnson and Abelman Jewelers?"

"Oh my," she said. "I haven't heard that name in forever."

"It just happens to be their emblem on the jewelry bag," Doreen said. "So I wondered if you maybe knew that store. They went bankrupt about forty years ago."

"And that would be around the time we found the jewels. Although it was probably not quite that long ago. Mack is thirty-eight already, so he was just tiny at the time of this discovery in the juniper. We told him when he was a teenager. Though I can't remember why."

"Okay," Doreen said. As it was now, Mack probably didn't even remember a word about it. Millicent had said something about him being busy at sports, but that didn't make any sense either. But then, Millicent's memory was not exactly something Doreen could count on.

However, the store going bankrupt about forty years ago potentially matched with the time frame Millicent had found the jewels. So that was all good. Figuring out who had owned the store and finding someone alive who still remembered and could provide a clue regarding who worked there would be difficult.

Doreen went through all the data she could find on the

store with various internet searches. The owners, the Johnsons, had been an old family name in Kelowna, and, when the daughter had married, the son-in-law had become part of the business. By all appearances they had been one big happy family. And yet Doreen knew things weren't always the way they appeared.

As she researched the second name, Abelman, she realized that was the son-in-law. They had been twenty-eight and twenty-seven at the time they got married, and only a few years later the son-in-law was brought into the family business on an equal partnership basis. But, as their only daughter, she would inherit everything anyway when her parents passed. That information Doreen had gleaned from the historical society.

Apparently Johnson and Abelman Jewelers was a highly regarded business, and the family had been extremely wealthy. The business had been failing and finally went under after the parents died unexpectedly, leaving the younger generation in charge. Apparently the son-in-law didn't have the same head for business that his wife's parents had. At least that was what Doreen surmised at the moment. Back then in the early eighties, diamonds were still a girl's best friend, but Kelowna wouldn't have been that large, so how much business would there have been for a prestigious diamond store?

However, the jewelry bag Millicent found contained more than just diamonds. Doreen studied the rest of the jewels, wondering what had happened back then. She did a search on the Abelman family and found Aretha and Reginald Abelman. Further research revealed that Reginald Abelman hadn't lived that much longer than Aretha's parents. He'd overdosed on drugs a few years later. Doreen frowned at that.

"That seems a little too convenient," she muttered. She headed back into Aretha's family history. She was twenty-eight at the time of her marriage and only thirty-eight when her husband died, so she would have been in her mid-thirties when the family business went under. So currently she would be seventy-five. Doreen sat back and smiled, reaching for her phone. "Good afternoon, Nan," she said cheerfully.

"Well, it's almost evening," Nan said, with a happy lilt in her voice. "I just came in from lawn bowling. A lovely game."

"Were you actually playing with the balls," Doreen asked, "or were you just betting on who would win?"

"Both," Nan said sternly. "It's good exercise."

"Good," Doreen said. "I was really hoping you weren't just betting against the winners."

"No," she said. "You've got to bet against the losers too."

"If you say so," Doreen said, rolling her eyes, because she knew Nan had never made a stupid bet in her life.

"I'm just about to head down for dinner," she said, "unless you've got a better idea."

"Oh, no," Doreen said. "I'll just sit here and have a sandwich at home."

"Did you finish all that zucchini bread?"

Since the zucchini bread had been given to Doreen days before, and Mack had been to visit several times, it was long gone. "I did," Doreen said, laughing, "but that's okay. I'm happy to have a sandwich tonight."

"You eat too many sandwiches," Nan fretted.

"No, I don't think so. Besides, I'm still not much of a cook yet."

"I've got some of my favorite recipes hanging around

here," Nan said. "I couldn't part with them when I left the house. I should just hand over the book to you. It's not like I'm cooking much anymore."

"If and when you're ready to get rid of it," Doreen said with a smile, "I shall be happy to have it."

"Did you have a reason for calling? Otherwise I'll go eat," Nan said. "All that exercise has given me an appetite."

"Right," Doreen said. "I was just calling to ask if you know Aretha Abelman."

"Aretha?" Nan pondered. "I know that name, but her last name is not Abelman."

"So who's Aretha?" Doreen asked.

"Her husband ran one of the little insurance companies around here," Nan said.

"Oh, that makes sense. She probably remarried."

"Yes," Nan said, "She and Hobart were together for decades."

As Doreen looked down at her notes, she realized that, even at thirty-five, decades into a second marriage was still quite possible. "Did she ever have a family?"

"No, it was always suspected she couldn't have any," Nan said bluntly. "Never really understood that myself."

"Some people's biology just doesn't work the same as everybody else's," Doreen said. "Really difficult if she wanted children."

"I don't think she wanted children as much as she wanted to have *had* children," Nan said with a laugh. "There's a very fine distinction there."

"True. Did she ever talk about being married previously or being part of a jewelry family?"

"All the time," she said. "It was one of the things she always reminded all of us," Nan said in disgust.

Hearing Nan's past tense usage, Doreen's heart sank. "Are you saying she's dead?"

"Oh, I don't know if she is or not," Nan said with a careless attitude. "The woman wasn't terribly nice. She always lorded it over us that she had more money than we did."

"But the jewelry company went bankrupt."

"That was after a robbery," Nan said dismissively. "She never considered that their fault. Somebody came in and stole a lot of their stock of jewels, and the insurance company refused to pay out on all of it because they just had a shipment brought in, but there was some confusion on just what had arrived."

"Wow," Doreen said. "For somebody who you don't really know, you sure have a lot of information."

"I didn't want the information," Nan said in a snappy voice. "You've got to realize she's the kind of person only interested in making you understand how she's better than everybody else."

"Where is she now?"

"No idea," Nan said with a sniff, her nose probably rising, as if Doreen had insulted her. "However, I could ask around and see."

It was so unlike her grandmother to be snippy about somebody that Doreen couldn't help pushing. "Were you rivals for the same man or something?" She wasn't sure what else to ask. But Nan's snorted disgust got her laughing. "I guess not, huh?"

"She married that stuffy Hobart," she said. "That man was a nightmare."

"But could he keep her in the style to which she was accustomed?"

"I don't know how they did it," Nan said, "but she certainly lived in a big highfalutin house. She had one of the first houses up on the Knox Mountain area, with a huge view of the city and a pool and the whole works."

"Well, good for her," Doreen said. She didn't have anything against a woman doing well.

"Yeah, but it's not like his little insurance company should have done that well."

"I don't know," Doreen said. "It seems like a lot of insurance companies do very well."

"Maybe so," she said. "But I'd be more than happy to help you try to find dirt on her."

"I'm not trying to find dirt on her," Doreen said gently, not willing to tell her about the jewels because, if Nan thought they would be returned to this woman, it might be the last straw for Nan. "I'm just wondering how that whole jewelry business went under. It seems that a robbery shouldn't take down a longstanding business like that."

"That's easy," Nan said. "Neither of them worked. At least not well. Neither had a head for business. She was involved in her father's business, but only in the sense that she was the model used for everything. They had a lot of different rings, and apparently she had gorgeous hands. Her father was very proud of his little girl, so she was in a lot of the advertisements."

"Which would have gone to her head, of course," Doreen said.

"Yes. But that still didn't give her the right to lord it over us."

"Of course not," Doreen said quickly. "How often did you see her?"

"Way too often," she said. "She was here at Rosemoor

for a while. And I used to pass her when I was coming back and forth to visit friends. But she hasn't been here since I moved in. Honestly, I'm not sure if I would have moved in here if she'd been here too. The woman is insufferable."

"Ah, Nan," Doreen said with a warm smile. "Please don't ever change."

"Not planning to," she said in a huff. "I'm not like Aretha." And, with that, she hung up.

"It would be nice if you didn't hang up on me, Nan." But her grandmother was gone before those words were spoken.

Chapter 3

Friday Late Afternoon …

DOREEN STARTED A file, writing down the information she'd gotten from her grandmother. Then she started looking for Aretha and her new husband. Had Nan mentioned a last name? She frowned at that. Hobart what? And what was the insurance company name? Doreen hesitated calling Nan again to ask. Her grandmother would know she was working on another case, and Nan could be relentless when she wanted information. Doreen researched online first, and it wasn't long before she came up with Hobart's Insurance Company.

Not exactly the most professional-sounding business name—and using his first name at that. But it worked. She brought it up only to find the business had been sold ten years ago. Hobart had lasted another three years after that, and then he died. After a little bit more digging, Doreen couldn't find anything new about Aretha. There was no sign of family, extended or otherwise, and she didn't have any children, according to Nan. So Aretha was apparently a fairly wealthy older lady who'd been alone now for several years. But where was she?

Doreen studied several more articles online and found that Aretha considered herself a bit of a philanthropist, as she donated to various causes. At the top of her list was always children, animals, and women's shelters. That made her a more likable woman in Doreen's eyes. But that didn't necessarily mean that Nan would like her. But why wouldn't she? It was so unusual for Nan to have such a pet peeve about somebody. But then, of course, Nan had come from no money and had built up everything she'd had on her own and had enjoyed life with a lot of different relationships. It was quite possible Aretha was a pious judgmental person. Doreen knew that could irritate Nan. It was also quite possible the two women had clashed over something else, like Nan's gambling, for instance.

There were any number of possible reasons why somebody didn't like someone else. And, as soon as somebody didn't like you, human nature being what it was, you tended to not like that person back. And what was it Nan had said? That the insurance hadn't paid out on a load of jewels that had come in. Were they really lost after that burglary? Or had that burglary been something set up that had gone bad? But then why would you burgle your own store? Particularly if the insurance wouldn't pay out. None of that made any sense.

But then how much were Aretha and her first husband really into the business anyway? Her parents apparently had built it up from nothing, starting it when her parents were in their early twenties. It wasn't until after their daughter had married that it hadn't done all that well. How much of it was Aretha siphoning off jewels and funds, potentially to keep herself in the lavish lifestyle she considered her right? Just because one owned the jewelry store didn't necessarily mean she was dripping in jewels.

Doreen herself had spent many an evening covered in jewels, but the minute she walked back into the house, her husband had removed them from her neck and ears and wrists and had locked them up in the safe. Even though she had received them as gifts for various anniversaries and other occasions, her husband had never let her have access to them otherwise. So when she left, she couldn't take them with her.

Annoyed at that, she started a list of all the jewelry her husband had given her, yet kept. Surely that wasn't right. They were supposedly gifts. There'd been a beautiful pearl necklace, an emerald necklace, a beautiful sapphire pendant, several rings and bracelets. She wrote down as many of the individual items as she could and wondered if she had any pictures of them. She had a lot of photos on her phone and then also on her cloud account, where she had kept them stored away and set aside for memories. Maybe that had pictures of the jewelry.

She would like it if Mack's brother could get just her personal possessions back. Surely her husband didn't have the right to keep those too. She didn't want to go looking online for pictures of him and his lawyer girlfriend, Doreen's divorce attorney no less, in case the lawyer was now wearing Doreen's jewelry. That would really suck. It also made her angry. Finally she got so angry that she snatched her phone and sent Mack a text about his brother.

You just contacted me about him today, Mack texted back. **I haven't had a chance to reach out to him.**

She sat back and sighed. Then sent a text back. **Sorry. I was just getting angry thinking about all my jewelry.**

What jewelry?

The gifts he gave me over the years, she typed. **I**

wasn't allowed to keep them. He locked them up in the safe every night. And, of course, I didn't have access to the safe.

And when you left, you left them behind?

No choice.

But they're yours?

He gave them to me as gifts, yes.

Wow, Mack added. **Not a nice man.**

No.

I'll mention it to my brother.

Okay.

And, with that, she had to leave it.

Her stomach growled. But the last thing she wanted right now was another sandwich. She stared around the kitchen, wondering if she could justify some Chinese takeout. She hadn't had any in so long. She got up and found the roll of bills Nan had slipped into the bag of veggies just a few days ago and opened it up. Another three hundred dollars in there. "Nan, you're such a sweetheart." Doreen could live for a whole month on three hundred dollars. Of course she had more bills coming that had to be paid, and that was a bit of an issue. She checked the fridge and winced at how empty it was, then closed it again.

She sat back down. "Well, if we walked down to the Chinese place to see what was on special," she said to Mugs and Goliath and even Thaddeus, "we would wear off the calories by the time we got back again." Likely cold too. And maybe she couldn't come inside with her animals, but she didn't give herself a chance to hesitate. She got up and grabbed her wallet, checking how much money she had, including the three hundred dollars, and saw way too much to be carrying around. She took out ten dollars and put it in her pocket, so she wouldn't spend more, and then put away her wallet.

With all the animals in tow, she headed out the front door, setting the security system, then down her driveway and around the cul-de-sac. She still had a way to go, but it wasn't too far.

A post office sat in the same little corner, as well as a pizza place and a gas station with a little convenience store attached. Such a beautiful evening to be out for a walk.

As she walked across the road, the traffic had slowed down, and the evening lights had come on. It would be really beautiful on the way back, if darkness ever fell, because the lights on the marina and the boats out in the harbor were visible from here. It was truly breathtaking.

Back on the other side of the crosswalk the four of them carried on for the next two blocks, and she finally turned in to the area where the Chinese food was. She headed toward the corner where the store was tucked into the back, but, as she walked inside, Mr. Fong Woo lifted his head and smiled, until he saw Thaddeus on her shoulder and the rest of her animals and got upset.

"No animals. No animals!"

She glared at him. "I just want to place an order, and then we'll wait outside."

He appeared mollified, until he saw the ten-dollar bill in her hand. He rolled his eyes. "Big spender."

"Not a big spender," she said, feeling a little defiant, "but it's what I have. What can I get for ten dollars?"

He looked at her in surprise, his fingers rapping away on the countertop, then snatched a take-out menu, placed it in front of her. He started to circle things. "Combo A, B, or C," he said. "Or you can have a single dish."

She nodded and stood here for a long moment. "How

about this combination?" she said. "Noodles and lots of vegetables and almond chicken."

He rang it up. "With tax it's a little over ten dollars."

She glared at him. "But it says in the front window that I get a ten percent discount if I pay cash."

He looked at that, smiled, and said, "I forgot." Then he changed the order and said, "Now you have enough," and handed her back a little bit of change.

She smiled and said, "We'll be outside." She pulled the animals back outside to a big area with a round concrete table across the way beside a health food store that served shakes and coffees too. She looked at her coins and sighed. "We didn't bring enough for a coffee."

Mugs barked at her, obviously smelling something he wanted in the nearby garbage can. She kept him on a shorter leash because other people were around. Goliath, on the other hand, didn't have that problem. He hopped up onto the big concrete table and sprawled himself on his side, his tail flicking in the late afternoon sun. She reached over and gently scratched his ears.

"I'm not getting anything for you to eat," she said. "Chinese food isn't for kitties." He just looked at her. Those golden eyes of his were mesmerizing. She smiled, then reached down and kissed him on the top of the head. He looked at her like she'd done something horribly wrong. She laughed.

Thaddeus took the opportunity to jump off her shoulder and hopped down beside Goliath, where the bird curled up against Goliath's belly and hunched down, so he was tucked against Goliath's underarms. She never really understood this move, but Goliath didn't even move.

She looked down at him and said, "You are a beautiful

kitty, and I thank you for not hurting Thaddeus."

Thaddeus gave her a strange little look and started to make a weird cackling sound.

She stared at him. "I really don't think I want to know what that means."

And he did it some more.

She groaned. "There should be a handbook on bird sounds." Then she realized there probably was one, and all she had to do was check the internet. She pulled out her phone, checked to see she had enough data, and then searched on sounds that African grays made.

The trouble was, they evidently had the ability to make hundreds of sounds, which she shared with Thaddeus. For whatever reason, Thaddeus seemed to think that was worthy of a chuckle. But sitting there, snuggled up with a cat who was likely to eat him, was hardly something to chuckle at. But, as long as Thaddeus was happy, she was good too.

She sat here, smiling, as she watched the pizza guy return, leave, and then come back again. "The delivery address must be pretty close for such a fast delivery," she muttered.

And while she waited, the health food store switched their sign from Open to Closed and even turned the lights down. She could see the woman inside, trying to cash out.

Just when she wondered if the Chinese food had to be grown before it was cooked for her, she heard a call from behind them. She turned to see Mr. Woo waving at her. She walked back inside and said, "Is it ready?"

He nodded and smiled, handing her a plastic bag. The smell was especially good. She grinned at him and said, "Thanks."

"You come again," he said.

"What if I only have ten dollars?" she asked wryly.

"You come with no money," he said, "we still feed you."

Surprised at that and touched, she said, "Thank you. That is very generous."

He shook his head. "You good people," he said. "We feed you." Then he disappeared into the back.

She could see all the slips of orders lined up by a kitchen pass-through window and realized he was in for a very busy Friday night. With the animals in tow again, she headed to the riverside this time and walked down Mission Creek. Then she had to cross over and come up around the corner. She headed up the back path to her property. She sighed happily as she reached home. She put the food on the little table outside on her deck, went into her kitchen to grab a knife and fork and a dinner plate, and poured herself a glass of water. Just as she sat down, she heard a voice call out.

"In the back," she yelled. Good thing she'd disarmed the security; otherwise no way Mack could come in. She scooped almost half of the Chinese food onto her plate, realizing it really was a huge portion, and she would have enough for tomorrow too. Except, with Mack here now, there was a good chance she wouldn't get any leftovers. He came storming through, but the fury on his face had her freezing in place.

"What on earth is the matter?" she cried out.

He stopped, took several deep breaths, and pinched the bridge of his nose. "I'm trying to calm down, but—"

"With you, it's never an easy process," Doreen said with a smile. "I'd offer you some of my Chinese food, but it's all I've got."

"And I'll say, *Thank you*, and take it," he said, marching back inside, grabbing a plate and fork.

She watched almost sadly as he scooped the rest of the

Chinese food onto his plate. "If I'd known you were coming, I could have ordered twice as much."

"I'm kind of surprised you had time to pick up Chinese food, since you've been so busy getting into my family's affairs," he said.

She stared at him in surprise, and then she knew. "Ah," she said. "I guess you talked to your mother, didn't you?"

He put down his fork very precisely, then glared at her. "What on earth did you say to her?"

"Nothing, why?"

"Well, she has suddenly decided you're the answer to everything, and you'll find out exactly who those jewels belong to." And then he stopped, leaning forward. "But what the hell are the jewels? Where did they come from, and what's this got to do with my mother?"

"Didn't she tell you?" Doreen couldn't imagine her only telling Mack a little of the story.

Mack shook his head. "Only that she had put you on to your next mystery and that you would solve something that had worried her for a long time."

"Wow," Doreen said, sitting back in surprise. "I think she just threw me to the wolves."

At that, Mack sat back and laughed. "You know what? She just may have done exactly that."

Chapter 4

Friday Dinnertime ...

DOREEN CHUCKLED. "SO, let me explain." Then she told him about his mother telling her about the jewels she had found years ago.

Mack stared at her. "How come I've never heard a word of this?"

"I was a little confused if you'd heard or not. One time she told me that you didn't know, but she also said something about having mentioned it to you, but you were always off doing sports. So, I don't know exactly what the deal was."

"I've been a cop for fifteen years," Mack said. "She had fifteen years to tell me."

"She did," Doreen said, as she picked up a bite of broccoli, then crunched her way through it and moaned. "Gosh, this is so good."

"You're not getting off that easily," he said.

"Me?" she said. "I didn't do anything."

"Where are the jewels now?"

"On my kitchen table," she said, "but you also must know that she did hand them over to the cops. They held them for thirty-plus days, so now they are technically hers."

"So nobody picked them up?"

"Nobody picked them up, and, not only that, the cops back then couldn't trace them."

"Right," he said. He shook his head and ate another large bite of noodles. "This is really good," he said. "Normally when I come here to eat, I have to cook first."

"And like I said"—she gave him a stern look—"if I'd known you were coming and were expecting to eat, I could have ordered twice as much."

"Good point," he said. "We'll want something for dessert to help fill in some holes."

"Maybe." She pushed back her empty plate. "I wonder if he gave me more than normal."

He looked at the container. "What did it cost you?"

"Nine dollars and forty-five cents—or something like that," she said, reaching into her pocket to pull out the change.

He looked at it and said, "That's a lot of food."

"I know," she said. "Maybe it was an overlarge helping. I don't know. He did say that, even if I didn't have money, he'd feed me."

At that, Mack chuckled. "That could be a really good deal for you," he said, shaking his head.

"And, of course, I could never take advantage of it, except maybe if I was super hungry and truly needed the food," she said quietly. "I'm grateful I'm not in that situation at the moment."

"Hey, speaking of jewelry," he said, letting her comment slide.

She appreciated the change of subject. The last thing she wanted was to have more discussions about her dire circumstances.

"The jewelry that your husband still has. Is it really yours?"

"I'm not sure how that works under the law," Doreen said, "but he gave them to me. Like the emerald was a wedding gift. The pearls were my birthday gift, and there were matching earrings. There was a beautiful sapphire pendant he gave me for an anniversary."

He just stared at her. "When did you wear them?"

She really hated to tell him this part. "When he told me to. Sometimes we argued about it because I'd want to wear a piece, and he wouldn't get them from the safe. Other times he wouldn't like my choice, and he'd want me to put on something else."

"Controlling, wasn't he?"

She nodded. "Very. I never had access to the safe, so I could never get the jewels out on my own."

Mack continued to eat.

Doreen, on the other hand, had finished all her food. But watching him eat made her hungry for a little more. "We shouldn't have eaten all the zucchini bread," she thought out loud. "Another piece of that would be perfect with a cup of coffee right now."

"Good," he said. "Take a look at what I brought, when you go in to put on the coffee. It's on the counter."

She looked at him in surprise, then jumped up and raced inside to see something wrapped up in tinfoil. She put on the coffee and brought out the tinfoil package, placing it on the outside table. "What's this?"

"Did you take any when you left?"

He was back to discussing her jewelry. She shook her head. "No. He refused to give me anything."

"So they were hardly gifts in his mind?"

DALE MAYER

"I'm certain they were always assets in his mind," she said. "He gave them to me, but, as long as he kept control of them, they were still his."

"Right," he said. "I sent an email to my brother about that. He was wondering if you had any proof of the individual pieces."

"How could I have proof of gifts?" she asked in a wry tone.

"Photos of the jewelry you wore?"

She looked at him in surprise. "You know what? I do have photos. I was thinking I should try to find some of those anyway."

"Because?"

"Because of exactly what you said. I don't know how to tell people those pieces are mine. Even if I tried to get some of them back, I don't have a way to identify them."

"Pictures would be a good start." He was still working away at the food on his plate.

"So, what's in the tinfoil?" she asked, nudging it.

He grinned at her. "Open it and see."

She unwrapped the foil to see cinnamon buns inside. Four big ones, each coated in icing.

"Oh my," she said. "Wherever did you get those?"

"Somebody bought a big pan in to work," he said. "That was left at the end of our shift, so I grabbed them. They won't be any good tomorrow anyway."

"But they'll be perfect with coffee tonight," she said in anticipation. "Good thing I shared my dinner with you."

"Good thing," he said. "Otherwise I might not have shared my dessert with you."

She chuckled. "Are they dried out from sitting on the counter all day?" She reached for one, but she didn't have a clean plate. She put it back down, hopped up, and went into the kitchen to return with two small plates. She cleared off the dirty dishes, taking them to the sink, while Mack cleaned up the take-out garbage. And when she got back out with two cups of coffee, she found two cinnamon buns on each plate.

"Two should really be too much," she confessed, "but I want them both anyway."

"And so you should," he said. "I keep saying you could use a little more weight on you."

"That's such a bizarre thing to hear after all these years. My husband would have been horrified to even see one of these on my plate. I'd have been lucky if I'd gotten one-quarter of one roll."

"Seriously?"

She smiled. "He controlled everything, including my dress size."

"Good Lord," he muttered.

"I know, and you're wondering why I stayed."

"No, I'm not," he said, "because I've seen it before. Once you're molded into who this person he wants you to be, it's hard for you to see that you were ever anything different."

"Well, I keep asking myself why I stayed," she said, "because that all seems so very different from who I am now."

"Don't worry about it too much," he said. "You are a very different person now."

"Thankfully," she said on a sigh. But, with a bright smile on her face, she looked at the cinnamon buns. "Do we need to do anything with them?"

He looked at her in surprise. "What would you like to do?"

She shrugged. "I don't know. I feel like a kid in a candy store because I've never had a whole cinnamon bun to myself before, and now there's two."

He laughed. "I'll put mine in the microwave for all of ten or so seconds," he said, "then I may cut them in half and butter them."

Doreen stared at him in wonder. "Now that sounds decadent."

"When you work hard," he said, "you get to eat well."

Mack picked up his plate and took it to the microwave. Doreen followed with hers. He put it on for about fifteen seconds. When it came out, he cut them in half and buttered the inside. The top half had icing, but the bottom half didn't. She did the same; then they took their plates back outside again. As they went out, she snagged the bowl with the jewels and the jewelry bag and her notepad and sat out in the fresh air with him.

"These are the jewels," she said, placing the bowl on the table.

He looked at them. "Are they real?"

She shrugged. "I don't know. I did figure out the bag came from a business called Johnson and Abelman." She showed him the emblem on the bottom of the bag. "That was their old logo."

He stared at it, then looked at her.

She shrugged. "They went out of business forty years ago," she told him.

At that, his eyebrows shot up.

"Somewhere around the same time these were found in the juniper." She looked down on her notes and tapped the pad. "This is what I got from your mom. She made notations of it in her gardening journals."

"And yet she never said anything," he murmured.

"I think she put them away in her mind, not just in her physical hiding place. She doesn't believe they are hers, so never sold them."

"They would have fetched a decent price," he admitted. "And they sure could have used the money."

"Maybe," she said, "but your mom never felt entitled to them."

"Of course not," he said. "So she gave them to you."

"With the request that I try to find the owner."

"Which won't be that easy, depending on the circumstances. It was a long time ago."

Doreen nodded. "The thing is, if they're hers to keep, they should be yours. And you aren't so wealthy that you should be turning away that kind of money."

He stared at the jewels, as if mesmerized. "Wow." He reached over and picked up the big ruby. "These are ready to be set, aren't they?"

"They are. But what I don't know is if they are real. I could take them down to the jewelry store and get them appraised."

"Good idea," he said. "So what else have you found out about them?"

She told him about the young wife turned widow who remarried somebody in the insurance business. Then she said, "Oddly enough, Nan doesn't like her one bit."

At that, Mack chuckled. "That could be for any number of reasons."

She explained what Nan had said.

At that, his laughter fell away. "People who have a lot of money and look down on others don't tend to have many friends."

"My grandmother is definitely not somebody who would tolerate that," she said.

"Nan had quite a lot of money stashed around this house," he said, looking at the kitchen and the rest of the house behind him.

"She did, but she wasn't interested in cash—or any of it, for that matter," Doreen said.

"Is she okay financially?"

"I keep asking her." Doreen shrugged. "She keeps laughing at me, tells me that she's fine."

"Well then, you don't have much choice but to believe her for now," he suggested. "Just keep an eye on her and make sure she is."

Doreen nodded. "That's what I thought." She stared at the jewels. "There was a burglary," she said suddenly.

At that, Mack put down his fork.

"But that was before the jewelry store went bankrupt. Apparently a new shipment of jewels had come in just before the theft, but there was a discrepancy on the jewels that arrived versus what was ordered. So they only got the value of the other jewels they had at the time."

"And you're thinking that's why they went bankrupt?"

"Well, if they got the insurance money to pay for what was there before, but they'd had a large shipment of raw jewels brought in," she spoke the words as she thought them, "it's quite possible the insurance money had to go toward paying off the creditors."

"That is possible," he admitted. "I don't remember hearing anything about that jewelry store."

"It was started by the husband and wife Johnson," she said, "until their one child, a daughter, married Abelman. He was eventually brought in as a partner only they were struck by a series of unfortunate events and within a few years everything went south in a big way."

"And that was forty years ago?"

She nodded. "The bankruptcy was not quite forty years ago."

"Do you suspect either were involved in the theft and insurance payout?"

"It is something to be looked into." Doreen frowned at him. "Any way to check back forty years to see if there is a police record of your mom turning in the jewels?"

"What would that do?" He eyed her carefully.

"I hate to say it, but your mom's memory isn't what it used to be," she said quietly. "It's possible she told the cops something more at the time. Something that's written into the case she opened up when she brought in the hidden gems."

"It's possible," he said, "but I don't know if the record is still around. But she's right though because, after thirty days, we do have to return found property."

"Unless it was involved in a theft maybe," she said.

"And you're right there too," he said. "So I wonder if it's simply a case of the cops couldn't prove it was part of a robbery because they couldn't trace them."

"Or ..." She stopped and stared at him. "What are the chances that ..." She paused again, knowing that, if she said anything more, it would piss him off.

"Chance of what?" He spoke in a hard voice. "That the cops were involved or something stupid like that?"

"Well, I guess the next question is," she said, "when Millicent got them back, were there ever any break-ins at her house?"

"Why would there be?"

"Because somebody found out she had the jewels back again."

"I have no idea," he said. "It's all just been dumped in my lap. I still can't believe you were the first to hear about it."

"Your mother brought it up out of the blue when we were talking about gardening," she said. "She just suddenly brought it up."

"There's something about you that has that effect on everybody." Leaning back, he stretched. "I can take a look and see. *Forty years back.* That would be in the files we have stored downtown. They're supposed to scan them all in, so they are digital, but haven't yet. There was an attempt to get started on that, but we just don't have the man-hours."

She nodded. "And something like this, with loose stones, if there's nothing to identify them?"

"Exactly. I'm not sure how something like these would be identified."

"I think," she said, "each jewel has its own identification, and maybe even a certificate, but, if there isn't anything that we can go on, I don't know what to say."

"I heard something about certificates, but I don't know if they had that back then." He used his finger to stir the dozen little jewels in the bowl. "It does look like it could be a lot of money," he admitted.

"I think it is," she said. "I understand jewels, even if I've never had the opportunity to buy or to sell them. And these look seriously expensive. I can't imagine they are fakes with that clarity."

"So, I'll look for the old records, and you look for any photos you have that show you wearing your jewelry. I know my brother is interested in seeing those."

"Sounds good," she said. "Have you seen all the materials we've collected for the deck?" When he shook his head, she wanted to hop up immediately, but she still had one-half of a cinnamon bun. "These are really filling," she said.

"If you don't eat both of yours," he said, "you can save one for breakfast."

She beamed and said, "That's perfect. I still have half of one, and that was the half with the butter on it." She sat here and drank her coffee. As soon as she was done, she hopped up and said, "Come see," and dashed around the side of the house, with Mack slowly trailing behind her.

He stood there and studied the collection and nodded. "We're getting there," he said. He leaned over and grabbed one of the green boards Arnold had brought and smiled. "These are perfect for stringers."

She stared at it doubtfully.

He looked at her and frowned. "Don't you think so?"

"I'm still trying to figure out what that board of wood has to do with string, why we're stringing it in the first place, or what a stringer even is."

He chuckled and made indents with his fingers, holding it upright at an angle. "Then we put the boards right here on each of those."

And then it clicked, and she could see the steps take shape in front of her. "*That's* what you're talking about. That makes so much sense now."

"It does, and it doesn't," he said. "We have to cut them all exactly the same, which is a little bit dicey because it's easy to screw that up. And it's not like I'm a pro at this or anything."

"No, of course not. But I trust you," she said. "And you won't make a mistake on purpose."

"Can it be a mistake if it's on purpose?" he asked curiously.

She hadn't a clue. She shrugged. "You said we still needed more hardware, right?"

"Yeah, but I talked to Chester. He helped his dad build a deck, and they have a bunch of metal couplings and stuff leftover. They would take them back to the store for a refund, but his dad hadn't bothered, and it's well past the deadline now. So he was okay to give it to us."

"That would be perfect," she said. "How much more do we need before we can get started?"

He looked at her in surprise. "We don't need tons more to start. We'll need more before you can finish though. You said you wanted to clean off the ground underneath the deck and maybe lay some tarps and gravel down to stop any weeds from popping through."

"Yes, but that wouldn't require good tarps, would it?"

"No," he said, "it doesn't. And those are pretty cheap. Princess Auto often has stuff like that around."

She didn't know what Princess Auto was, but she was willing to listen to him. "So, are we talking this weekend, this month, or next month?"

"Good question," he said. "I would suggest we could do some of the rough work this weekend. If you want to grab some tarps," he looked at the area and continued, "you'll need a couple of ten-by-twenty, or at least ten-by-ten tarps to get in here. Probably more, depending on how much of the area on the side of the house you want to just put rock down on."

"I wouldn't mind having the whole side of the house done. I did hear about somebody that put mats down," she muttered. "That would be nice too."

"Yes," he said, "but lots more money."

"But rock on top of a tarp like this," she said, "isn't that slippery?"

"It can be." He nodded. "We can put down crushed rock. Then we can take a packer and flatten it. That's always good to do."

"It depends which is the cheapest."

"Right now we don't have to worry about the side of the house," he said, "and we can't really do it until the deck is done anyway because we've got all the material sitting here."

"Good point," she said. "And we don't need rocks on top of the tarps yet, if we put the cinder blocks in and around. We're building a floating deck so we can just grab enough big rocks to keep the tarp in place for now."

"Exactly," he said. "So, if you want, my Sunday afternoon is free. I can come over and start placing some of these big concrete corners and get them leveled off. Depends on when we'll get the hardware, which we're waiting on Chester for."

Frowning at that, he pulled out his phone and sent a text to Chester. When he got a response right away, he smiled. "Chester is heading out on a date right now, but he'll bring stuff by the station in the morning."

"Perfect," she said. "So maybe what we should do is go out Sunday at noon, as soon as you are free, and get the rest of the stuff we need."

"We'll see," he said. "I remember talking to Larry, one of my neighbors. He said he had a bunch of stuff sitting out in the backyard, just turning brown in the sun."

"You can talk to him too. We don't have to do it this weekend, if there's any hope of getting more parts and pieces. I'd love a deck, but I really don't have the money for it right now," she admitted.

"Right," he said. "Besides, there's just something very satisfying about getting a job done for minimal money."

"Oh, it's not just me who feels that way, huh?"

He chuckled. "I think everybody likes a bargain. In a case like this, it's an even bigger bargain."

"Right." She gave him a big smile. "So, the next thing to do is to see just what all the parts and pieces are. I'm getting impatient."

"Let's see what Chester brings tomorrow, then I can always look at my neighbor's leftovers and see what he's got. If need be, I can bring stuff over tomorrow too."

"I feel really bad," she said. "You're doing so much for me."

"Yep," he said, "but that's all right. We help each other in this world."

She felt really sad over that because, in her world, so many people hadn't been the kind to help. "I really appreciate it," she said suddenly.

"Don't worry about it. Remember? You shared your Chinese food with me, and I shared my dessert with you. So it goes both ways."

She chuckled. "Good point, and it was really good, wasn't it?"

"Yes," he said. "Now, I better head home. It's been a very long day. Thanks for dinner. If you want, we can do lamb chops tomorrow."

She beamed. "Or Sunday, if that's better?" She followed him through the house and out onto the driveway.

He frowned, then nodded. "Maybe Sunday would be better. I'll stop and pick some up. Then we'll cook them Sunday."

She smiled and nodded. As he was pulling away, she muttered, "Can you have lamb with pasta?" She knew if she could get him to cook another huge pot of pasta, she could eat all week without any problem.

Plus she knew that, given a chance, she would eat pasta every meal.

Mack gave a honk on his horn and drove away, with a hand waving out the window. She waved back, feeling a sense of loss and loneliness as he left. She had really gotten used to having him around daily when she fell through her little bridge again recently. But she'd see him again soon. Boy, it was good to have him in her life. She turned and walked back inside.

Chapter 5

Saturday Morning ...

SATURDAY MORNING DAWNED bright and clear. Doreen hopped out of bed with an energy she wasn't expecting. Just the thought of starting on the deck expansion tomorrow was huge and exciting. She was a little worried about the cost involved. And what if she got a little way into the job and then had to wait until she had more money? That would be tough, especially since she couldn't collect any money yet on the sale of the antiques or even the sale of Nan's clothes.

Mack hadn't left her any money for the gardening she'd done on his mom's yard. She groaned. She knew it was because he was so busy with work. She wished she could help him out, but unfortunately she was a large part of the reason he had so much work to do.

In the kitchen she put on her morning coffee, disarmed the security system, and opened the kitchen window and the back door. The animals all barreled out. Thaddeus flew out the window, as if he couldn't possibly make it fast enough out the door. She shook her head.

"What's up with you guys?" she asked, stepping onto her little deck to look around. But there was nothing to see.

Except that the water was definitely higher. It was bobbing close to the top of the path now. She stared at it in surprise. Looking back at the coffeepot, she realized the first cup was almost half dripped and wondered if she could steal a cup because she wanted to go down to the creek herself, coffee cup in hand.

She had put away the jewels in her bedroom last night, wondering what to do with them. She needed to get the appraisal done, but she didn't know how long that would take. She wasn't comfortable leaving the jewels anywhere but at home with her. She also wasn't happy at the idea of showing anyone else the jewels. Secrets had been buried with the jewels, and, if opened, all heck could break loose.

Finally, she managed to get a cup of coffee from the still dripping pot, and, with the animals crowding around her, she walked down to the creek. It had risen at least eight to ten inches overnight. Was more to come? If that was the case, her pathway was about to go under. It was still quite a bit lower than her backyard, but wow. Mugs kept going closer and closer to the edge.

"Mugs, stop," she snapped placing her full cup on a big rock.

He looked at her and woofed, then, almost like a two-year-old, took one more step toward the water and darned if he didn't start to fall. Doreen raced to his side as he scrambled up the bank, trying to get back out of the heavy rush of water. She managed to snag him by the collar, just in time to pull him toward her. But, as a result, she ended up falling on her own butt, sliding down toward the water. It was all she could do to hold herself back from ending up in the fast current herself.

She could hardly see through the surface; the water was

dirty, as if it had picked up dirt every inch of the way as it headed down her little creek to become a river. She remembered seeing aerial photographs of the lake, where the brown rush of water from the river flowed into the lake and left this big half circle of brown as it stirred out to the middle of the lake. And that was exactly how the pickup truck with those poor people had ended up in the lake in that big crush of high water some years back.

This was nothing compared to that, but it was enough for her to have a reality check. She looked around and noted that, if the water kept rising like it was, she couldn't take the creek route to Nan's anymore.

She shook her head. "Who knew?"

Mugs scooted back a couple feet and sat beside her on her property but on the little bit of a hill area, so she could watch the water. Thankfully he missed sitting on the newly transplanted heather.

"It's so beautiful but so deadly." Just then she heard a voice from over Richard's fence.

"Like all water," the voice snapped.

But whose voice? His? His wife's? Doreen was never sure who she was talking to when she had no face to put to the androgynous voice. Richard had said he was married and that his wife's name was Sicily. Yet Doreen had never seen her. The mystery of Richard's partner remained unsolved to date. But Doreen's curiosity hadn't dampened.

She stared at the fence. "Can you see? The creek is so high."

"It's not that high," he/she said. "It's not coming under my fence yet."

She stopped and stared, thinking about that. "Does it normally get that high?"

"Not normally," the voice said, "but I've certainly seen it happen a half-dozen times in the years I've been here."

"I understand better now," Doreen murmured. But then her neighbor's fence was a little lower too. So maybe that made sense. "Well, I no longer have a fence, so I can see it while I sit here on my property."

"You can watch it all you want, but it can get dangerous as all heck."

"Wow," Doreen said. "I'm really amazed." The early morning sun was shining on the water that danced and gushed all the way down to the lake. "It's incredible." Branches floated by and even occasionally a whole tree. "There has to be thousands of gallons of water plugging through here."

"Yes," the neighbor said.

After that, there was no more conversation, as Doreen just sat and enjoyed herself. Finally her coffee cup was empty, so she turned and headed back to the house to get more. The ground itself seemed a little wetter, as if the water had soaked in through the ground overnight, reaching back toward the house.

The water was coming out of the hoses she had hooked up to the sump pump with Nan's help. She stared in surprise to see just a trickle coming out, but it meant the pumps were working. She headed over and lifted one of the round wooden disks above the pump to see water on the inside.

Even as she watched, the pump activated, sending a gush of water that was in the little cistern out to the creek. She smiled. "Wow," she said, "there's more to this than I expected. Does everybody have pumps along here?"

But the neighbor didn't answer. She figured that either he/she was down at the creekside or had gone into the house.

After the handcuff case scenario, it wasn't like the neighbor was any friendlier. It was almost as if he/she had decided to blame Doreen for all that attention. But, so far, the media hadn't heard about the pink satin handcuffs found in Richard's front garden. Too bad. They could haunt him for a change.

She was still chuckling as she headed up to the deck and inside. She really should make a trip to the local jewelry store, get a receipt for all the jewels, and leave them for an appraiser, if it seemed okay with them. She grabbed the loose stones in the jewelry bag. She still wasn't terribly comfortable with the whole appraisal thing. She also needed to go grocery shopping and might even come back with tarps, so Mack's time off could be spent doing the stuff she didn't know how to do.

It would take her a while to figure out the tarp thing and to pull the weeds. She wasn't sure about getting rocks in just yet, as plenty of rocks were around her garden, and, of course, if she wanted to, she could always pick up a couple from her creek. There was probably some law or something against it, but, if she was careful and not too greedy, maybe the city wouldn't mind if she removed a few of them.

Picking up her purse, she reset the alarm, and leaving all three of the animals inside, she stepped out. Mugs hopped up on the door, trying to tell her with his barking that he wanted to go with her. She called back through the door, "Sorry, buddy. I can't take you in the grocery store, and I'm not leaving you in the car."

She went to the hardware store first and found the cheapest tarps. Only at twelve dollars, they were not exactly cheap. She hesitatingly put them back on the shelf, wondering if there was a better option. She texted Mack.

Where's that place you said is best to get tarps?

He responded, and she remembered the name, although who in their right mind would put "princess" in the business name for an auto shop? She found her way to what looked to be a military and outdoorsy all-in-one-guy type of store. She walked inside to find an older man with a bald head smiling at her.

She looked up at him and grinned. "Okay, I know I don't look like I belong here," she said, "but I'm looking for tarps to put under a new deck we're trying to build."

"Perfect," he said with a nod, then led her to the tarps. "These are pretty cheap," he said, "particularly for what you'll be using them for."

"I don't want weeds to come through," she said, "so I don't want it to be too cheap."

"Not a problem," he said. "The material is really dense. You could also double up on them, if you wanted."

"How much are they?" she asked.

"They happen to be on sale this weekend." His smile was genuine. "It's buy-one-get-one free, so it works out to be two for ten bucks."

Delighted with that, Doreen picked up two, then she stopped and looked at the size and said, "They're ten by ten."

"Is that how big your deck is?" he asked. "Or bigger?"

"Bigger." The trouble was, she didn't know how big the end result would be, and she didn't want to shortchange on the tarps.

"When you get the concrete blocks tucked in," he said, "make sure you dig these down, otherwise you'll get weeds around the blocks."

She frowned at that and nodded.

He continued, "And you could grab a third one and cut up pieces to extend it."

"Or do you have the bigger ones on sale too?" Doreen asked craftily.

He chuckled. "I do have some that are twelve-by-fifteen."

"I'll take two of those," she said. "I can always fold under any surplus."

They were fifteen dollars, but, hey, she would take that. With both tarps in her car, she headed to the grocery store. She didn't have much money with her because she deliberately didn't budget much for each week. But she needed a little bit more than she had planned for. Including coffee. As she wandered the aisles, filling her basket, she thought she heard her name spoken. She turned around to look, but nobody was there. Then she heard her name, not being called, more like someone mentioned it in a conversation. She moved closer and heard several older women having a discussion about *Nan's granddaughter, Doreen.*

As she came around the corner, somebody nudged one of the others, and they all shut up. Doreen looked at them and smiled. "Did I hear you talking about me? I thought I heard my name mentioned. *Doreen?*" She'd always found the best way to deal with gossips was to nip it in the bud.

One of the women looked at her, then raised an eyebrow, her nose going up in the air. "Of course not," she said. "Why would we talk about you?"

The arrogance and such a superior tone in her voice stopped Doreen, and she looked at her in surprise. "No reason, I guess," she said, easily hiding behind her years of training with an equally arrogant husband. "Of course, if you're gossiping about anyone," she said, "it's really not well looked upon, is it? My grandmother is a lovely person, so I know that, if you're talking about her, it would be in the best regard."

The whole time she spoke, the woman glared at her.

Doreen just gave her a sunny smile and walked to where the bananas were. She picked up one banana and put it in her basket.

"Is that all you can afford?" the woman asked.

Doreen could feel anger sparking inside her. She turned and slowly looked at the five women gathered together, and only one had the grace to look ashamed. The other three were backing up the older woman.

"Of course not, but waste not, want not," she said with an airy wave of her hand. "You must be Aretha."

Shock slammed into the woman. "How do you know who I am?" she demanded.

Doreen gave her the smallest of smiles. "It's really not hard to figure out," she said, and she moved to walk away, but that wasn't enough for Aretha.

"What are you talking about?" she said. "Tell me!" Then she reached out with a birdlike hand that was all claws and gripped Doreen's arm. "How dare you talk about me!"

"I haven't talked about you." Doreen could lie with the best of the snobbery club, if called upon. "But I did hear you were a little too arrogant for your own good and that you looked down on everybody else if they didn't have as much money as you did," she said with a laugh. "So it was immediately obvious who you were. And, of course, these are your sidekicks. I'll be sure to find out who they are too."

With that, she simply smiled at them all and, ignoring the shocked look on Aretha's face, said, "Have a great day, ladies!" She pushed her cart forward, and, as she walked past them, she could see some men who worked at the store looking at her with their jaws open. She gave them both a bright sunny smile and said, "Remember to never lower yourself to the level of those you can't stand."

And, with a laugh, she carried on to the checkout stand.

Chapter 6

Saturday Morning…

S TILL CHUCKLING, AND having seen the wide-eyed gazes of the cashiers and everybody around them, Doreen pushed her cart out to her car and loaded the few groceries she had bought, including her single banana. She never was one to have many bananas around because they ripened so fast. Not that she was an expert on them, and maybe there was a way to stop it, but it seemed like bananas went from green to black in split seconds, particularly during the heat. The last thing she wanted was a whole pile of black bananas that she didn't know what to do with.

On the other hand, the incident had been very eye-opening in terms of Aretha's personality. But Doreen had met many women like her. Doreen's previous life had been fraught with women who were all so much better than she was. Or at least they wanted to be. In her case, her husband had been an all-powerful figure, and many times those women, in particular, wanted nothing more than to be her.

As she got back into the vehicle, she really wanted to chuckle because Aretha would be so surprised to know about the jewels Doreen was taking to get appraised right now.

Inside the vehicle Doreen drove to the largest of the jewelry stores in town. It was located inside the mall, which was not her favorite place, but, if that was where they were, that was where Doreen was going.

As she walked inside the mall, she headed toward the jewelry store and asked to speak to the manager. The clerk looked at her in surprise, then shrugged and went into the small back room. Very quickly, two women came out. The older of the two smiled.

"Hello. What can I do for you?"

"I'd like to get some jewels appraised, please."

"For insurance purposes?" the woman asked, pulling her glasses off the top of her head.

"That's part of it, yes," Doreen said, as she glanced around. "I would really prefer not to have everybody know what I've got."

"Of course," the woman said. She lifted a portion of the counter. "Come with me."

Together, they went into the back of the store, where a small table was in an office area. As soon as Doreen was seated, she pulled out the little bag and handed it over. "I've obviously photographed everything at home," Doreen said, "but for insurance purposes and identification, we need more detail."

The woman nodded and carefully poured the jewels into a small sparkling heap on the table. She didn't make a comment, just studied them carefully. "I'll have to get these off to a specialist," she murmured.

"You don't have anybody here?"

"Not for some of these," she said. "*Hmm.*" She frowned. "Although, we do have a couple dealers here for a convention," she said. "I might be able to get one of them to have a look this weekend. I'll just send off a quick text, checking on availability."

That complete, with her finger she gently spread out the jewels so she could itemize what there was. She separated off the ruby, several emeralds—one larger than the others—and a small pile of diamonds, including a yellow diamond. "These are quite lovely," she said.

"I know," Doreen said. "Is there any way to identify them beyond taking a photograph? Are there any certificates or anything like that for jewelry?"

The woman shrugged. "Some have identification. Some have marks, and others come with a certificate of authenticity." She glanced over her glasses at Doreen. "Do you have any of those?"

Doreen shook her head.

The woman frowned. "So, I have to ask. Where did you get these?"

Doreen felt defensive. "You don't have to ask," she said smoothly. "And I'm not telling you right now."

The woman tapped her fingers.

"They're not stolen, if that's what you're asking," Doreen said, "and feel free to talk to Corporal Mack Moreau from the RCMP detachment."

The woman's eyebrows shot up at that. "So, the police know you've brought them in?"

She nodded. "Yes, it was their suggestion that I get them appraised, as well as checking to see if there is any way to identify each piece."

Frowning, obviously curious, and wanting more information, the woman picked up one of the larger jewels and, with her special loupe, examined it. "It is a rather spectacular piece," she admitted. She set it back down and frowned as she stared at the collection.

"When you say, *spectacular piece*," Doreen said cautiously, "about how much money would something like that be worth?"

"Well," the woman said, "I can't say for sure, but I feel confident saying this piece alone would be over twenty thousand dollars."

Doreen nodded quietly. She wasn't surprised, as she'd seen some very expensive jewelry of her husband's—although it still seemed like that jewelry should have been hers. "Okay, so I'd like a receipt for these, so I know everything is accounted for," she said, standing up.

"Of course, we can do that," she said. The woman brought a pad of paper toward her to make notes and then took photos, moving the images to the digital receipt she wrote up.

Doreen looked at her and frowned. "So you are insured for this if I leave them behind. Correct?"

The woman nodded. "Yes, of course, although we don't have a value established yet."

"So then how long for the appraisal?" Doreen asked, not liking the idea of leaving the pieces behind if they couldn't ascertain a value for insurance purposes.

The woman looked at her just as her phone rang. She picked it up and answered, identifying herself as Mindy Karsten. Doreen half listened to the conversation as she separated the jewels a little more so she could count them.

Doreen took more photos of the jewels in front of her. She finally realized they were talking about somebody coming back to the store to look at these very jewels.

When she was off the phone, the woman looked up. "You're in luck. He's coming over anyway and will be here in a few minutes, if you want to wait." Reaching for her pad and pen, again she said, "It'll take that long for me to wrap up this receipt anyway."

"That sounds great," Doreen said, then sat quietly in her seat, watching the woman carefully as she took several photos of each of the pieces and carefully added them to the digital receipt.

When a commotion at the front counter occurred, the woman looked up and smiled as a man walked around the corner and into her office. "Jeremy, how lovely to see you," she said, reaching up and shaking his hand.

He just smiled as she introduced Doreen, who immediately stood and shook his hand.

"So, what's this, my dear? You have some interesting jewelry? Is that what I'm hearing?"

"Jewels," Doreen corrected. "Cut but not set."

His brows came together. Mindy, the woman she'd been dealing with, stepped to the side. He sat down, pulled out his loupe, and looked at the jewels, picking out the biggest emerald. "Excellent quality," he said. "Obviously we're not talking the top tier, but these are very, very nice gems." He looked over at her. "Where did you get them?"

Doreen gave him a bright smile. "I don't wish to disclose that at the moment. What I'm looking for is an appraisal on the pieces. And to ascertain if there is any identification for them."

"You do, of course, have proof of purchase and possibly certificates, don't you?"

His tone was starting to grate on her nerves. She smiled and said, "Again, that's none of your concern. I was just speaking with Mindy about some aspects of this process. I don't know you from Adam."

He frowned, shaking his head.

"Don't frown at me. You might be a pro in your field, but I don't know you. I came here looking for an appraisal on these gems. Can you provide that or not?" she asked, getting irate.

His fingers went down to almost cup the jewels with some reverence.

A possessive reverence she didn't like. "I don't think you're the right people to handle this appraisal," she said. "Obviously, this is probably too sophisticated for you."

"What are you talking about?" he blustered. "But I do want to make sure they are your property."

"That is not within your mandate," she said smoothly.

He stared at her in outrage as she placed her hand over the jewels. She grabbed the jewelry bag and very carefully scooped them in, counting them as they went in. With all of them now secured, she looked back at Mindy. "Obviously the receipt won't be required." She looked over at the two of them and said, "You weren't very much help. So if you don't mind, I'll be leaving."

"You can't just walk out with those," he said, standing.

She stared at him and very quietly asked, "Why not?" She pulled out her phone and held it in front of her, as if she would make a phone call. Instead she put it on video.

"Because they're very valuable."

"Says you," she scoffed. "You certainly couldn't give me an appraisal on them."

"I need time," he said.

"Maybe so," she said, "but I don't like that you feel you have the right to question me. And I don't like your attitude. I'll find somebody else who can appraise these."

"We're the best in town," Mindy said. "I'm sure we can

help you."

"All you've done so far," Doreen said quietly, "is covet what I brought in. And that makes me uneasy. So excuse me, but no thank you."

"Would you want to sell them?" the man asked.

Doreen looked him straight in the eye. "No, they are not for sale." And, with that, she turned and walked out.

Still inside the mall, but away from the jewelry store, she could feel the tremors starting to move outward. They'd started when he'd arrived and had gotten much worse when she realized how much he really wanted those gems. It didn't matter how good they were, there was something about them that she could see he wasn't happy about. Something was very wrong here, and she exited the mall and headed for her vehicle. Feeling somebody watching her, she kept looking around.

As soon as she got to her car, she walked past it and pulled up to another vehicle, then crouched, as if to get inside. Then she peered around the corner of the vehicle beside her, and, sure enough, there was the man from the jewelry store.

She waited, watching as he came toward her. Then she raced around several vehicles farther away and brought up her phone again, taking another video. He got down to the edge of the vehicle she had supposedly gotten into, and he realized nobody was there.

Frowning, he stopped, then stood with his hands on his hips and looked around. She caught him on the video nice and clear, but, since he wasn't doing anything wrong, he would likely just say he'd come to give her another chance in a different environment to not feel so threatened and to possibly sell him the jewels. Then he pulled out his phone and talked to somebody at the other end.

That made her frown too. Why was he calling somebody else? It had to be about her and the jewels. She was outside of the mall now but presumed security's jurisdiction included the parking lot as well.

She needed Jeremy to get a long way from her vehicle, so she could leave. He slowly walked back to the mall, still talking on a cell phone. As soon as it was clear, she dashed to her vehicle, started it up, and pulled away, going in the opposite direction of where he was, even though it was closer to go home the other way.

This time she headed straight home. There were other things on her list to do, but this one had been unnerving enough.

In her driveway, she pulled into the open garage. Using the fancy-schmancy door closer Mack had given her, she waited until the garage door closed completely. As soon as she got out, she snatched up the jewels and her purse, then headed inside.

Mugs dashed around her, like she'd been gone for days. Goliath sat in the corner and yawned. She crouched and gave Mugs a really good greeting. "I should have taken you with me," she murmured. "He wouldn't have appeared so threatening if you were there to defend me."

With Mugs finally calming down, she put down her purse and the jewels, then went out to her car to get the few groceries she had just bought. It didn't take long for her to put those away, now wondering what her next step would be. Obviously, something about these jewels had caused a bit of a ruckus. She pulled out her phone, and, while she made coffee, she dialed Mack's number. It rang and rang while she ground beans and filled the coffeemaker with water.

When he finally answered, his voice was distracted, and noise was in the background. "Doreen, what's up?"

"You on a case?"

He sighed. "I'm a cop, Doreen. I'm on all kinds of cases. Is everything okay? Why did you call?"

"Because something weird happened at the mall today." She proceeded to tell him about the appraisal, or *nonappraisal* as it were.

"Interesting," he muttered. "His reaction wasn't normal though?"

"No. There was a certain adversarial nature to his gaze, and I know this sounds ridiculous but an almost possessiveness to his fingers. I didn't like it one bit, so I snatched up all the jewels, and I left as soon as I could. But get this. He followed me out to the parking lot, all the way down to the end, to where I'd pretended to go. Luckily I had ducked, so had come up a few rows away," she said, "but there's no doubt he stopped right where he thought I would be."

"Did he threaten you in any way?" Mack's voice deepened sharply.

"No," she said, "not directly. He just didn't like that I walked out with the jewels."

"Do you have his name?" She gave it to him, and he nodded. "When I get back to the office, I can take a look."

"Sure," she said, "I know you're busy."

"I am." And again his voice had that distracted note.

In the background she could hear somebody calling his name. "Oh, you have to go," she said hurriedly. "I didn't mean to take you away from work." With that, she hung up.

Pocketing her phone, she poured herself a cup of coffee and stepped out onto her little deck. Her tiny little short-term deck, soon to be replaced by one that was big and beautiful. If she sold any of the jewels, she would have enough money to redo the whole house probably.

But they weren't hers either. She understood how Millicent felt about them. Just because something was in your hands doesn't mean it was yours to do something with. She was certainly glad Mack knew about them.

Chapter 7

Saturday Midmorning ...

S PEAKING OF MACK, Doreen should have asked him to look into the old files on the break-in from the jewelry store from way back when. There might have been an inventory, and maybe these jewels were listed. But that didn't make sense because, when Millicent had turned the jewels into the police, they should have run it against any jewels they had listed as stolen from the jewelry heist or other crimes anyway.

Still, she wanted to check for herself. She didn't want to think that maybe the cops hadn't done their due diligence back then, but things happened. Just because Millicent said she had turned them in, was it her or her husband who went? She hated to think either of them could have said they had done something but hadn't. People did all kinds of stuff, though she knew she was walking a thin line because these were Mack's parents.

She sat here with a notepad, idly doodling and looking in her garden, trying to figure out what plants to put where, hoping maybe she could collect flowers and transplants from all different places, instead of having to buy them. Not only were mature plants so much more stable and easier to grow if you got offshoots from them but the nursery plants were often delicate and didn't handle transplanting that well.

She wasn't sure what the soil was like here in her own backyard, and, sure, a truckload or two of topsoil would be lovely, but it wouldn't happen anytime soon. As it was, she wanted stepping stones instead of a worn-down path all the way to the end of the backyard. She needed to cut the grass again too.

As she looked in that direction, she sighed unhappily and started a work list. Finish digging up the garden, weeding to the right side of the house, mow the lawn, trim around the new garden area, lay down tarps. At that, she brightened because she did have the tarps, so she could get those down now.

With that, she bolted upright. She was getting hungry; after all, she only had coffee for breakfast. But the thought of making another sandwich, after just going to the grocery store, didn't sound good to her. *I'll fix something in a bit*, she thought, as she sat outside, looking over the area where she would put down the tarps. That shouldn't be too hard to get done today. And, of course, it was so much more interesting than doing the weeding.

She glanced back to the side of the house, and her shoulders sagged. "That's the problem with doing stuff yourself. It doesn't get done unless you do it." If she had her slew of gardeners, it would have all been done in a couple days. Then she could have gone along and been superpicky about weeds still growing in the center of the plants.

But she was much less critical nowadays. It wasn't that she'd wanted to be critical back then, but, when you had a whole army of gardeners to keep busy, it seemed like the thing to do. Now she knew so much better.

She wondered about Aretha and how her wealthy lifestyle was working out for her. Doreen knew firsthand just how cold and empty it could be. Aretha had to be closer to Nan's age. But regardless of her age she still didn't look happy. That pinched look to her lips and the sallow, hollow cheeks that went along with that highfalutin skinny lifestyle didn't reveal any kind of rosy glow or inner joy on her face. Doreen wouldn't be at all surprised to find out the woman was extremely unhappy and depressed most of the time. A part of Doreen said she should reach out and try to be a little nicer, but another part said to forget it because the woman deserved everything she got. But that wasn't Doreen's way, unfortunately.

Determined to accomplish something, she got up and grabbed her gardening gloves. She called the animals out to the garden. She was determined to do some weeding at least.

Wandering down to the overgrown bed, she figured she could handle about ten feet without too much stress. Then she would figure out what needed to be weeded where the tarps would be.

With that, she grabbed her digging fork and wheelbarrow and headed to the spot she was working on. She should have brought some music out, and, almost as if reading her mind, the neighbor on the far side—not Richard's—turned music on. Some symphony. Not something Doreen would have chosen, but, hey, it was better than nothing.

As she listened to the music of an era long gone, she dug, rocking and rolling as she tossed weeds and picked up big rocks and moved them off to one side. She wanted the rocks, but she wanted to place them strategically when she was done, so she had a pile of big rocks in the garden and left the little ones where they were.

She really did need some topsoil, and that would be a problem. She could get one of those giant bags, maybe delivered with equipment over into her backyard, but that had to be at least one hundred dollars, if not twice that. And somehow she would still have to wheelbarrow the dirt in and out. She would probably need one bag for each side alone.

Groaning at the extra cost, but knowing the garden had been severely depleted over the years, she dug back in and kept coming up with more and more roots. She was working to get the roots under the base of the weeds, not just ripping them off halfway.

By the time she'd worked down the bed a good five feet, she realized how much she'd overestimated her abilities, particularly in the growing heat. She wanted to stop and go in for some ice water, but, at the same time, she knew, if she stopped even for a few minutes, she would quit for the day. She kept digging, and, by the time she was almost there to her ten-foot mark, she heard a voice calling out to her.

"Out here," she yelled back, and it wasn't long before Mack came striding through the kitchen. He stood at the deck. She lifted her very last shovelful, bent down, and shook all the weeds loose, reaching farther to loosen up some more that were deeper, and then heaped the ground around the plants. She straightened up, groaning. "I forgot how hard this work is."

"Maybe so," he said, looking down at the bed along the fence. "But you're doing a hell of a job."

She beamed at him. "Well, that's the established garden," she said. "I didn't really want to lose it, but it needed some work. I'd like to find a way to put something along the very back against the fence to stop it from rotting and to also give the whole thing more definition."

"We could probably put some loose boards along there," he said. "That would allow you to build the dirt a little bit higher along the back too." He walked down the few steps and came around to where she stood. Looking at the wheelbarrow, he asked, "Where are you dumping all this?"

"Out in the compost bin closer to the front," she said. "I was just bringing the bin down here to fill it, but now it's too heavy."

He gave a short bark of laughter. "I'll go dump it for you." He turned and grabbed the handles of the wheelbarrow as if it were a tiny toy and wheeled it ahead of her.

She raced past him and opened the big compost barrel near the garage. It was picked up every second week, and this one was definitely full. When he brought the wheelbarrow around, she used her shovel to scoop the contents from the wheelbarrow into the bin. "What are you doing here anyway? You sounded superbusy earlier."

"I am," he said. "A bunch of cases have been opened, and a bunch converged," he said.

She looked up at him and raised her eyebrows. "Can you tell me more?"

He shook his head. "Hell no," he said. "We have enough work to do without you getting in the middle of it."

She snorted. "On the other hand, if you told me about it, maybe I could cut your work in half."

He raised his eyebrows. "Are you insulting us?" he drawled.

"No, just poking a little fun." She snapped the compost bin closed. "Thank you. That can go back to the garden now."

Obediently he turned and pushed the wheelbarrow back

to where he'd found it. "Are you doing more this afternoon?"

She shook her head. "No. I planned to do that ten feet I just finished, then spread out the tarps and figure out the markers I needed to cut out that part of the lawn and get that done. But it took way more to do the ten feet of weeding than I was expecting."

"Ya think?" he said. "You'll need some more dirt in here, won't you?"

"Yep," she said. "Though I'm not sure how, or how much it'll cost."

"Especially back here." He frowned. "You can't get a dump truck in here. He could dump it on the driveway on a bunch of tarps, but you'll have to wheelbarrow it around."

She nodded. "What about those big bags they can sling around? Do you think they could drop it alongside the garage here or even around the back?"

He looked at her in surprise, then walked to the side of the house, frowning. Then he nodded. "You know what? They just might. At least that would keep it all contained, and you could just shovel out a wheelbarrow full at a time."

"That's what I was wondering," she said. "Then I could take it down, start at the far end, and work it back. But it would probably take at least two bags."

"More, I think, if you want to do both sides."

"I do," she said, "and I should top dress this grass in the center, but I wanted to get some patio blocks along in the middle because walking on the grass isn't the best."

He nodded. "We were talking about a patio in here." He looked at her. "Where are those tarps you bought?"

She beamed at him. "Let me go get them." She dashed up the steps and noted a full cup of coffee sitting on the railing. She glared at him. "Do you ever buy your own coffee?"

"Nope," he said, "I don't have to. I just come here and get a cup."

She rolled her eyes, snatched up her own empty cup, and walked inside. Thankfully there was still a cup for her, but it was cold. She groaned and put on a fresh pot, then checked his cup and found it cold too. She poured them both into a carafe and put them in the fridge. Iced coffee was a lovely thing in the afternoon.

While she waited for the fresh coffee to finish dripping, she went out to the garage, grabbed the two new tarps from her car, and took them out to where Mack was.

"Where's my coffee?"

"It was stone-cold," she announced. "That pot was made a long time ago. So I stuck that in the fridge and put a fresh pot on."

"Okay," he said. "You're forgiven."

She shook her head. "The nerve," she sputtered.

He looked at the tarps with interest. "Hey, I like these," he said. "They'd be great for camping."

"These will be great for under the deck," she snapped.

He chuckled. "There is that too. So what is it you're hoping to do?" he asked, as he opened one and spread it out.

"That's quite big, isn't it?" she said, studying the size.

"Maybe, but not quite big enough, depending on what you're thinking."

"I was just thinking to keep some of the weeds down below the deck, so they don't poke through."

With that, he took the digging shovel and put a quick line all the way around the outside of the existing deck, then another quick line for the space they were looking at outside the tarp, and yet another line to mark the space they were looking at for enlarging the deck.

"It'll go a little bit bigger than this," he said, "but it wouldn't hurt to have a bit of a ridge around here. We'll have to level off the blocks anyway."

She nodded. "While we have it marked, I could cut out all this sod. The compost bin gets picked up Monday. So I should fill it tonight, take it out so it is emptied on Monday, then I can put whatever is left of this sod into the bin on Tuesday."

"That's not a bad idea," he said, and he picked up the shovel again and started slicing it deeper so she could pick up sections of grass and move it. "This section will be tough." He motioned at the part of the lawn where she stood. "But, as you get closer to the house, it should get easier."

"Do you think I should just leave it in place and let it die instead?" She frowned, looking at it.

"Your choice," he said. "We'll have to dig the blocks down, and you only have what looks like maybe one step all the way around. Because the deck itself can't be too high. I'm afraid any longer grass will poke through."

She groaned. "It's just so much work."

"Since when are you allergic to work?"

"I'm not," she said, straightening her shoulders, fortified by the compliment in his question. She grabbed her digging fork, and, while Mack cut cross pieces, she used the digging fork to lift them. Then she beat the pieces a couple times with the digging fork to loosen them and tossed the pieces into the wheelbarrow.

Before long they had a good four-foot strip done. "That went fast," she said, surprised at the difference having help made.

"Big jobs are easier with more hands than just your

own," Mack said. "Even if just to know you're not alone in it."

She thought about that and nodded. "It seems like I've been alone a lot in my lifetime."

"Well, you're not now," he said. "You have a community, and that makes all the difference. Speaking of which. Did you find anything else about the jewels?" he asked.

She shook her head. "No, but I was thinking maybe you could pull the old records from that burglary. Presumably when your mom turned the jewels in to the police, they checked the jewels against the jewelry heist and didn't find anything that matched. I'd just like to confirm."

He nodded without saying anything.

"But it was a long time ago, so I don't know what you'll find for records," she continued.

"I don't know either," he said. "We do have paper records, and some of it's been scanned in, but most of it hasn't. It's just been sitting in storage."

She shook her head. "That makes no sense to me."

"Mass digital conversion," he said.

She nodded. "Well, let's hope something is there. Other than that, I had a not-so-interesting conversation with Aretha in the grocery store today." Then she filled him in on that exchange.

He looked at her in surprise. "At least you can hold your own," he said. "You understand women like that."

She nodded and reached up to wipe the sweat off her brow. "But you know something? The more I think about it, I don't think she's as rich as she seems. She didn't wear one piece of jewelry. After all those years of owning a jewelry store. Her clothing showed age. I remember the crimped look on the jacket that wasn't supposed to be there. Almost like the grand old dame had run out of steam and money."

"And now you'll be sympathetic toward her, I suppose." He gave her a big smile. "You try to be tough, but you're such a softy."

She gasped at that, muttering, "You're the softy. So who died?"

"A little old lady," he commented.

She stared at him. "Murder?"

He glared at her.

"Well, it must be, if you're involved."

"Other deaths come under my umbrella too, you know."

"What exactly does that mean?"

He shrugged. "When someone dies, and the person isn't known to have any particular health condition, we take care of the case until we get back the autopsy results. If nothing is suspicious about it, the case is closed. However, if something is suspicious about it, then we work the case."

"Is it a little old lady that Nan's likely to know?" Doreen jammed her digging fork into the ground with a little more force than she needed.

"Maybe," he said.

"Any connection to my jewel case?"

"*Your* jewel case?" he said in a teasing note.

She flushed. "Okay, so maybe it's not a case. But, if it isn't, then I might as well start looking into serial killer Bob Small."

"Hey, that's not funny," he said.

She shrugged. "I won't be bored, and that's been sitting in the basket. I'll have to deal with it eventually."

"Or not," he snapped, digging harder and faster.

She watched in amazement as he crisscrossed his shovel into the ground, making it so much easier for her to remove the sod. "I almost hate to be nice to you," she said with a grin.

He ignored her and kept barreling through the work. By the time he got half of it done and was well on his way to the two-thirds mark, she was enjoying it. He stopped and looked at her. "What's your problem? You look like the cat that ate the canary. Why?"

"You," she said, finally laughing out loud. "To get all this yard work done, I only need to get you steaming mad, hand you the shovel, and, boy, do you plow through it!"

He glared at her, then looked at the amount of work he'd done, and, despite himself, he chuckled. "Did you do that on purpose?"

She shook her head. "No, I sure didn't. But I'm happy with the result."

"Except you're the one who will have to shake out all that sod," he said, "and you're way behind now."

She nodded. "I get that, but I've already done a lot of work today. I can finish it tomorrow."

Just then Mack's phone beeped, and he looked down and frowned, headed for the house.

"What's the problem now?" she asked, following him.

"Another old lady," he said sourly.

She stopped. "Dead?"

"You didn't hear that from me," he said, "and, no, I don't have any details, so don't bug me."

"Got it," she said slowly. "It's an interesting conundrum, isn't it?"

"What?" He walked into the kitchen and poured a cup of coffee. Wiping his face with a damp paper towel, he said, "I've got to go."

She called back, "You really want to talk about it, but

you can't. That's the conundrum."

"I really don't want to talk about it," he said, "but you won't leave me alone. That's the conundrum."

She laughed and whispered, since he was gone already, "Good point, Mack. Good point." She knew she'd be racing for the newspapers as soon as she got inside to see what was going on with these little old ladies. It just added to her day.

She wondered if either of them were Aretha. That would be sad because, in Doreen's heart, she knew the lady was lonely and desperately in need of a friend.

Maybe Mack was right. *I am a softy*.

Chapter 8

Saturday Late Lunchtime ...

B ACK INSIDE, DOREEN was definitely hungry now as she
looked at the meager ingredients in her fridge, even
after her recent trip to the grocery store, and groaned. "I
don't want yet another sandwich, and I had just coffee for
breakfast," she said. And it was Saturday, so Mack wasn't
due to cook today. He was coming back tomorrow to cook.
So what the heck would she do in the meantime? Spotting
the eggs, she hadn't had an omelet in forever, and she could
make a good ham and cheese omelet. She wondered about
adding mushrooms and thought, if she sliced them super-
thin, it might work out. Nothing wrong with having an
omelet for a late lunch.

As she got everything out for the omelet, she sliced the
mushrooms as thin as she could and cooked her omelet,
putting the thin layer of mushrooms on before she folded it
over, then put a lid on to let the cheese melt and the mushrooms cook. When it was done, she was happily surprised to
see the mushrooms were just the way she liked them. She
served herself a plate and sat down at the kitchen table with
her laptop.

No mention of the deaths on the local news yet. But, when she went to one of the online newspapers, she found an interesting note about a body discovered. It didn't say it was an old lady though. Curious about that, Doreen clicked through to see if there was any more information but found nothing.

She wondered if she could now get an address for Aretha. Just something about her struck a chord. Doreen had met so many women like her, and, if not by the grace of God, Doreen could have ended up the same way herself down the road. But, as it was, she would end up more like Nan now. And that was so much more fun.

As if hearing her voice, Nan called on the phone. "Did you hear?" she cried out.

"Hear what?" Doreen asked.

"They found a body."

And her voice dropped to such a hushed yet excited whisper that Doreen had to settle back and roll her eyes. "People die all the time, Nan. That doesn't mean anything is suspicious about it."

"Oh, so you've talked to Mack already, have you?" And Nan's voice dropped with disappointment.

"He told me about it, yes, but they don't know if it's suspicious or not."

"Of course he does," Nan said, brushing that off. "That's just Mack, trying not to give you any details."

With a surprising start, Doreen realized Nan was correct. It was such a Mack thing to do. "Well maybe," she said, "he has good reason."

"Of course he does." Nan laughed. "He's trying to keep you out of trouble and away from his case."

"I'm not that bad, surely."

"Nope," Nan said, "you're much better than that. So, when you do find out, let me know, huh?"

"Will do," Doreen said. "By the way, do you know where Aretha is now? I met her at the grocery store today."

"Oh. right. I heard about that."

"What do you mean, you heard about it?"

"One of the five ladies there happens to live here at the home."

"Which one?"

"The one who tried to turn away," Nan said comfortably.

"How do you know she tried to turn away?"

"Because she always does whenever there's any conflict."

"Definitely one lady was trying to separate herself."

"Yeah, that's Hillary," Nan said. "She doesn't do well with conflict of any kind."

"And yet she's Aretha's friend? That must expose her to conflict on a regular basis."

"They were all part of the same group way back when, and they still make a point of appearing in public together. But honestly, I don't know how much the word *friendship* comes into play with that group," Nan said.

"I've got the feeling Aretha is just a lonely old lady," Doreen said thoughtfully. "One who has seen better times."

"You could say that for a lot of people in here," Nan said. "You really can't put too much stock in appearances."

"Maybe not, but I have to admit, as I sit here and look back on the conversation, I feel a little sorry for her."

"Don't get caught up in that," Nan said, sounding alarmed. "She's not friendly."

"No," Doreen said. "A lot of unhappy people aren't."

"Oh, dear," Nan said. "I was afraid of that."

"Afraid of what?"

"You're just too soft-hearted," she said.

"Maybe so, but, if you can tell me where she lives, I could take a drive-by, and that might put my mind at rest."

"I doubt it, but maybe if you're lucky it will." Nan rattled off the street name not too far away. "She's staying with a friend of hers who owns a big mansion. It's just the two of them there."

"Oh, interesting. So it's one of those old regal estates then?"

"Yep, exactly," Nan said. "Likely Rosemoor was just not good enough for her," she said in a scoffing tone. "Which is just crazy, as you know, because it's wonderful here," and her voice warmed up considerably.

Doreen smiled. "You're good for that place too," she said.

"Darn straight I am," Nan said. "Everybody here would die of boredom if I wasn't around."

At that, Doreen had to chuckle. "As long as you're staying out of trouble."

"Of course I'm staying out of trouble," she said, "and, if you want to come down, I've got more veggies for you."

"That would be great," Doreen said. "Maybe we will walk down now, since I just finished eating."

"Good, I have some walnut bread. Do you know how many walnut trees grow in the Okanogan area? There's so many. And hazelnut bushes. And it's definitely not the season."

"Don't they have to dry first?"

"Sure," Nan said, "but then everybody has all their old nuts to get rid of, so they can make room for the new ones. Come whenever you're ready," and she hung up.

Doreen put the phone down as she thought about Nan's words and realized there really was some logic to it. But it was a little weird to think about. She looked at the animals. Mugs had been watching her since he'd heard Nan's voice on the phone. Doreen looked down at him. "You want to go see Nan?"

"*Woof, woof!*" Mugs barked, dancing around her.

She looked over at Goliath, who was sprawled out, sound asleep, on the chair beside her. She reached out a hand, scratched his belly, and, as she went to withdraw, he grabbed her hand and pulled it back to his belly.

She chuckled. "You can stay here all alone, or you can come to Nan's with us." He dug his claws in, not allowing her hand to leave his belly. "That's not an answer," she said. "Or not an answer I'm prepared to live with."

Thaddeus, who had been sleeping on the window ledge, lifted his head and gave his whole body a shake, so his feathers stuck out at all angles.

Doreen laughed at him. "Don't you look beautiful, gorgeous."

"Thaddeus is gorgeous. Thaddeus is gorgeous."

She chuckled. "That's a new line for you, but I'll have to agree. You are gorgeous."

He hopped down and preened from one side to the other. "Thaddeus is gorgeous," he said in a singsong voice.

"Thaddeus, can you sing?"

He gave a cackling sound, like a witch, that made Doreen stop.

"My goodness," she said. "Where did you get such a wonderful range of sounds?"

Thaddeus hopped onto her hand, the one on Goliath, then reached down and pecked at his belly. Goliath made a *meow* sound and bolted off the chair.

Doreen looked at Thaddeus. "You did that on purpose," she accused.

He looked up at her, gave a *he-he-he* and then broke into song. "Thaddeus is gorgeous."

Doreen picked up the leash and hooked up the squirming Mugs, who was dying to get out of the house. "What's wrong with you guys?" she scolded. "We've been outside all afternoon."

She opened the kitchen door, then remembered the alarms. She headed back to the front door, locked it, and set the security system on the kitchen door as she left that way. After all, she had the jewels here with her. With the animals ahead, except for Thaddeus, who had taken his perch up on her shoulder and was still busy singing about how gorgeous he was, she walked to the creek, wondering if she could get another trip down the path.

In contrast to earlier, the water level had dropped slightly. She smiled at that and walked toward her grandmother's place. She couldn't imagine anything better on a Saturday midafternoon than lounging about, doing some gardening, and visiting with friends and family. It was something she'd missed all those years she was married. Her husband had refused to let her have much of a relationship with her grandmother, and her friends were his friends that he deemed appropriate. She remembered when a couple divorces happened among his group of friends; she had been told clearly not to have anything to do with the wives.

Thankfully they had never contacted her afterward anyway, but she often wondered now what she would have done. Back then she didn't have much of a personality because it had all been subdued under what was right and correct and precisely how her husband wanted it. That was the problem with being molded and marrying so young.

But thankfully she wasn't that way now. She was her own person and enjoying every bit of it. Of course that didn't mean she wanted something to happen to her ex or his current girlfriend, her ex-lawyer. Come to think of it, Mack hadn't mentioned his brother at all when she'd seen him. But then he appeared to be quite distracted with this new case.

Who would have thought Kelowna would have been this busy little city of criminals? But, as she thought about it, over 140,000 people lived here within the city limits, and some of these crimes had been spread over multiple decades, so it wasn't such a high crime rate. But still, Doreen seemed to be the one finding them all.

Maybe she did have a knack for it. Or maybe she was just a nosy busybody, like some people thought.

She was no sooner around the corner when she saw Nan waiting for them. She lifted a hand and waved and realized for the first time she wouldn't have to argue with the gardener. She walked across the stepping stones, feeling as if something were lost. "Nan, whatever happened to Fred?"

Nan shrugged. "Seems he lost his job. At least in the interim until the trial."

"I'm so sorry for all that," Doreen said.

"Of course you are," Nan said with a beaming smile. "That's because you have a good heart."

"It's possible he might get off with a much lighter sentence," Doreen said. She hated to admit maybe she was okay with that too.

"Maybe," Nan said, "but the law has to run its course now."

"If only he hadn't had a part in all of it."

"Well, he did," Nan said, "so don't you worry about it."

Doreen laughed. "It's not like I can't worry about it."

"Sure you can. You have to learn to manage what it is you'll worry about. If I worried about getting old, I'd expend all my energy on something I couldn't stop. So I'd rather spend my time making each day lovely." She smiled. "Come sit down. The tea is almost ready." And in a voice a little more commanding than usual, Nan said, "Now!"

Surprised, Doreen grabbed her chair and sat.

Chapter 9

Saturday Late Afternoon ...

"WHAT'S THE MATTER, Nan?"

Nan grumped a little bit, as she puttered around, bringing out teacups and a plate of what appeared to be the walnut bread she'd spoken of earlier.

Doreen wasn't sure what had happened, but Nan was obviously upset. "Nan?"

Nan turned and shook her finger. "I don't want you involved with that Aretha person."

Surprised, touched, and a little upset, Doreen settled back and asked, "Why not?"

"She's the poisonous kind," Nan announced.

"Maybe she was," Doreen said quietly. "She looked very unhappy."

Nan glared at her.

"So, you want her to still be a bad person?" Doreen asked gently, as she poured the two cups of tea. "Or is it that you're upset at the idea maybe she's not who you thought she was?"

"She was very mean to some friends of mine," Nan said. "They didn't deserve being talked down to like she did."

"Did she ever talk to you like that?"

Nan shook her head. "She tried a couple times, but I have more backbone than to allow it."

"And some to spare," Doreen said with a smile. "But the thing is, I've met lots of women like her. And they're very unhappy on the inside. I also think she's lonely."

"Maybe so," Nan said, "but I'm warning you. She's poison, and that's all I'll say on the matter." She gave a quick nod, as if to add punctuation to her comment.

Doreen kept her smile hidden. "I highly doubt she'll have anything to do with me anyway."

"Good," Nan replied. "Surely you have another case you're working on by now."

"Do you know anything about missing jewels?" Doreen asked in a bright tone.

"Missing jewels?"

She nodded. "Yes. Jewels that are missing."

"I don't know why I would," Nan said.

"Oh, I'm just wondering if you know of any case where somebody lost a little jeweler's bag full of cut but unset gems."

Nan frowned as Doreen pulled out her phone and brought up the pictures she'd taken. "Oh, goodness, aren't they lovely?" Nan said with a bright smile. "They really are beautiful."

"They are, indeed. But we also don't know who they belong to."

Nan just stared at her. "That's hardly something you'd lose."

"It's certainly possible," Doreen said.

"I don't know how." Nan looked at the bag. "Do you know anything about the jewelry bag?"

"Johnson and Abelman," Doreen said without hesitation.

"Right, you mentioned the store earlier. Those are truly beautiful. Seems like, if it was a theft or from when the store burned down, there would be records."

"Wait. The store burned down?" Doreen asked, staring at Nan over the rim of her teacup. Her grandmother was in possession of some of the darndest information.

Nan nodded. "Yep, it burned down just before they declared bankruptcy. They had to at that point. They had nothing left. The insurance company, suspecting fraud over the missing jewels claim, dropped their coverage. I think the parents were still trying to get the place reinsured when it went up in smoke. They lost everything. They died not long after."

"That's terrible," Doreen said with a snort. "Was the fire an accident, I wonder? Too bad the parents aren't still alive to ask who knew about the insurance being canceled. If no one knew, then maybe it was deliberate to save the business. But, if everyone knew, maybe it was deliberate to finish off the family business. Then again, it might have been a terrible accident."

"Exactly," Nan said, "but I'd put that fire down to Aretha's first husband. He was really kind of useless."

"It does seem like he drove the business into the ground." Doreen thought about the stately Aretha; maybe she had taken a step down in life after all. Maybe, by the time her husband died, there hadn't been any money left.

"No, he wasn't any good at business," Nan said with a smile. "And Aretha was a girl who liked to wear the jewelry."

"Do you think she had anything to do with the burglary?" Doreen asked.

Nan looked at her, surprised.

"Oh, my goodness," Nan said. "I can only imagine what kind of a scene that would have been, if she had."

"Exactly," Doreen said. "So, you're saying the business burned down soon after that?"

"Yes. It was very soon after that," Nan said. She shook her head. "Well, I hadn't heard any of this about the jewels."

"It doesn't change much, but it does make you wonder," Doreen said.

"Yes," Nan said. "Maybe it is *poor* Aretha after all. I can't remember now," Nan said. "Did her husband commit suicide? I think there were rumors to that effect." She tapped her jaw as she tried to remember.

"If he did, maybe it's not so hard to understand, given the fact they were broke."

"But the insurance should have covered a certain amount."

"Depends on how much they had the business insured for," Doreen said. "And insurance companies don't like to pay out."

"No, of course not," Nan said. "It's money going in the wrong direction, as far as they're concerned."

"Exactly. ... Of course, if her husband committed suicide fairly soon afterward ..."

"I know that look on your face," Nan said eagerly. She leaned closer. "What are you thinking about?"

"Not a whole lot," Doreen said. "It's just interesting. I'll have to look up her second husband."

"Well, he's dead too," Nan said with a wave of her hand, as if to say, *Easy come, easy go.* "There isn't a lot you'll learn about him."

"Does he still have family around?"

"Of course. His brother is here," Nan said.

"Brother? What brother?"

"Mangus. He's in here with me. But he's older, and he's also kind of a grump."

"Sounds like maybe he's of the same mold as Aretha." Doreen was clearly distracted, her mind going in all directions.

"I don't think there's been any love lost between them," Nan said. "When they were both here, they wouldn't even sit at the same table."

"If I was still married, and my husband died, and I came to Rosemoor, I'm not sure I'd want to hang out with my husband's old friends or family either."

"Okay, good point," Nan said. "That could very well be it. Aretha doesn't do well with anybody. You know that, right?"

"That's what you keep telling me," Doreen said with a smile.

"Just say that you believe me," Nan said.

"Okay."

The conversation eased back a little bit at that point.

"So, what about Mangus?" Doreen asked. "Is there any way I could talk to him?"

"Probably," she said. "You could come by on Monday. He's on my lawn bowling team."

"Are you enjoying the game?" she asked curiously.

Nan laughed and nodded. "I am and finding it fun," she said. "I'm not saying I'm very good at it, but Mangus is quite good."

"Is he here now?"

"Nope, he's not. He's gone away for the weekend."

"Interesting. How does one get away for a weekend

when in Rosemoor?"

Nan snorted. "Honestly, he's probably gone into the hospital for a procedure. Anyway, he's not here and is supposed to be back Monday."

"Good," Doreen said. "Maybe I can talk to him then."

Nan nodded, then looked at her watch. It was about the third time she'd looked at it.

"Am I keeping you from something?"

"My favorite show is coming on."

"Oh my," Doreen said. "I don't want to put you out."

"It doesn't matter," Nan said. "If I miss some, I'll just pick it up later."

"Maybe, but I'm totally okay to walk home now."

"If you're sure?" Nan frowned at her.

"Absolutely," Doreen said. "Besides, the tea's all gone."

At that, Nan started to laugh. "Good point. It is, indeed." She stood. "Would you like some walnut bread to take home?"

"I'd love some," Doreen said warmly. As Nan walked back into the kitchen, Doreen wanted to mention the vegetables she'd been promised, but, at the same time, maybe Nan had given them away to the others.

Then Nan came back out and set her basket down. "Pick the vegetables you want, please," she said. "I'm honestly struggling to eat it all."

"I don't want to take too much," Doreen said, but eyed the huge tomatoes with a gleam in her eye.

Nan chuckled and pulled out a plastic bag. "Here. Let's get you some cucumbers and carrots. Green onions of course. Oh, and some tomatoes." Very quickly she closed the bag, nearly emptying the entire basket, only leaving herself one tomato, a couple small baby carrots and a little lettuce.

"Nan, are you sure?" Doreen asked, looking down. "You've only got a little left."

"Not only am I sure," Nan said, "but here. She held out a tinfoil-wrapped packet. "Six slices of walnut bread. Feel free to share with the good detective, if you'd like to."

"He's cooking dinner tomorrow night," Doreen confessed. "So I'm sure he'll love some."

Nan literally rubbed her hands together with glee.

Doreen frowned. "Don't read too much into this," she warned.

Nan's face drifted off into a smooth and unlined innocent look that didn't fool anyone.

Doreen laughed, then leaned over and kissed her grandmother on the cheek. "Thank you, as always."

She called the animals and walked over to the flagstones, still feeling odd that Fred wasn't around, then started her walk back up to the curb. She stopped and looked around, but Nan had already gone inside.

Doreen looked down at the animals.

"Time to go home, guys."

Chapter 10

Saturday Evening ...

BACK INSIDE, DOREEN carefully put away her fresh veggies and the walnut bread. Now she had an address for Aretha's home, but, more than that, she also had a brother-in-law from her most recent husband's family.

She sat down at her laptop and did some research, but she felt restless now. The evening yawned before her, but she couldn't get rid of the feeling that she should check out where Aretha was living. Doreen mapped out the place and discovered it was only about six blocks from her home.

"If only we'd known that," she announced, "we could have gone directly from Nan's place."

Packing up the animals again, she headed out the front door and took a shortcut that ended up taking her around the block, so only about four blocks were left. She was there in no time. Happy that she'd come this evening so she didn't have to fuss and worry about it later tonight, she stopped outside the beautiful mansion with the big locking gate.

The place reminded her of the home belonging to Ed Burns. That was the case where the nasty son Jude had his father killed so he could take over the estate. This estate before her wasn't as grandiose and definitely wasn't worth the same amount of money, but still it was a lovely home. As Doreen looked at a bit of garden she could see from outside the fence, the gate opened, and a woman who'd been gardening stepped out and smiled at her.

"Hi," Doreen said, with a beaming smile. "I was just admiring the garden."

"You're Doreen, aren't you?" the woman said.

Doreen was startled. "How did you know?" she asked, but the woman just laughed.

"Because of the menagerie that came along with you, of course."

Doreen looked down to see Mugs wandering through the beautiful daisies in the garden. "Oh, gosh, I'm so sorry," she said. "Mugs, come here." She tugged on the leash. Mugs dropped his butt and looked at her, as if to say he wasn't interested.

The woman smiled. "Not to worry. He's more than welcome in my garden. I'm Heidi, by the way."

"Oh, I'm so grateful you don't mind," Doreen said. "Some people definitely do."

"Not at all," Heidi said.

"I wish I had some lovely plants like these," Doreen said. "I'm redoing my nan's garden. Well, it's my garden now, I guess I should say. But I don't have much in the way of perennials."

"Come on in and take a look," Heidi said. "I'm weeding out plants right now. Because I have so much, they've all become overcrowded."

Doreen looked at her in surprise. "Have you got any to share?"

"Oh, boy, do I ever," Heidi said. "Come on inside. I'm

not even keeping all these bulbs this year. If they survive the winter, they survive. Otherwise I'll be pulling them."

The bulbs she talked about were dahlias. Doreen stood in front of a beautiful purple dinner plate dahlia and gasped. "These are stunning," she murmured.

"I'm really happy with them. But you know what the tubers are like. They multiply quickly."

"They do," Doreen agreed. "Should you ever have any extras, I would love to put some in. I have one section of the garden I could literally do all in dahlias."

"It's too early to pull the tubers, as these haven't even flowered yet," she said, "but I still have lots left over from last year. I didn't even bother putting them all out."

The two women walked the garden, which was amazing. Painted daisies, echinacea, white daisies, and black-eyed Susans, just to name a few. Doreen had a little bit here and there but nothing like this. Some red plants she didn't recognize crawled along as ground cover.

"Wow," she said. "This is a superior garden. I would love to have this many plants."

"You're more than welcome to come back tomorrow. I'll be pulling a bunch of each of these," Heidi said, "because everything is just too thick." She pointed to some. "See? I've already pulled these."

Doreen walked over to see multiple plants. Perennials from snowball bushes that were small and obviously volunteers, to a small hydrangea, and all the daisy-like flowers she had just looked at. Turning to the lady, she said, "If you don't want these, I would be more than happy to take them."

"I would love that," the woman said. "I do hate to kill a plant."

Doreen nodded. "Do you happen to have a bag I could put these in?" she asked. "As you can see, I'm out walking. These animals and I walk all over town."

"So you should. It's great exercise. Let me have a look inside." She disappeared into the big house.

All of a sudden yelling came from inside.

Doreen frowned and looked down at the animals. Mugs wasn't happy at the noise and had been sitting quietly beside the wheelbarrow, but now stared up toward the house, barking.

The woman came out looking a little shaken.

"I'm sorry. Is there a problem?" Doreen asked hesitantly.

The woman looked at her, giving her a slight shake of her head. "No. Just a little resistance I wasn't expecting."

"Oh, dear," Doreen said. "I'm so sorry."

"It doesn't matter. Here. Let's see what we can package up for you to carry." Very quickly, Heidi had everything from the wheelbarrow slipped into two bags. She gave them a light shake to see if they were too heavy. "What about these? Do you think you can carry them okay?"

"Oh, I'm sure I can," Doreen said, giving the woman a bright smile. "I can't thank you enough."

Then she noticed another small bag the woman had brought out and handed it to her.

"These are all dahlias," she said. "Like I said, I never even had a chance to get them in the ground, but they are a mix. I can't tell you what they are. I never really cared and always thought of it as the joy of planting."

"Oh, my word, thank you."

"I haven't had a chance to go into my gardening shed yet, so, if you want to come back tomorrow, I do have more bulbs. I would take them down to the local church bazaar, but, if you would like some tulips or hyacinths, I mean, really, I have so many plants here." She looked around almost helplessly at a garden that had gotten completely overgrown while she wasn't looking.

"I am overjoyed and very thankful to have anything you want to move out," Doreen said. "I have at least sixty feet of garden I'll fill."

The woman gasped in joy. "Oh my, that will be stunning."

"Well, it will be," Doreen said, "but it certainly isn't yet."

"If you had a car—" She stopped and looked at Doreen, who was nodding.

"I do."

With a nod the woman smiled. "And how about a shovel? If you could bring a shovel in your car tomorrow, we could fill bags and buckets and give you some of these." She walked through, pointing out dozens and dozens of plants she wanted to move out.

"I would be ecstatic." Doreen was filled with gratitude in her heart. "This would make my garden so full and abundant from the very beginning."

"They'll have a little bit of trouble transplanting at this time of year, but, if you cut them back, they'll grow next year."

"Absolutely," Doreen said, and, with that, the two women arranged to meet the next morning. With a happy wave, Doreen turned to head back out again.

As the gate closed behind her, she turned, startled at the unexpected noise. Aretha stood on the front step, her hands on her hips, glaring at Doreen. She lifted a hand and called out, "Nice to see you, Aretha." Lifting the plants, she said,

"Heidi was kind enough to pass these on to me."

Heidi whispered, "Don't you worry about her. She can be cranky, but she's really a good person on the inside."

Doreen nodded. "Isn't it sad how sometimes the niceness has to hide on the inside because there's so much fear of letting anybody see it?"

"Yes," Heidi said with a bright cheerful smile. "I'm really glad to see you understand. She's been living with me for a year now. We've had some issues, but she's really a nice person."

"Lovely," Doreen said, and she meant it. "I'm looking forward to seeing you tomorrow morning."

With that, she set off, heading back home again. The walk was enjoyable, but the plants were heavy. It hadn't looked like too much when she'd started, but, by the time she made it back to her place, they felt seriously heavy.

Once back home, Doreen walked around to the back and put the plants down in one of the ditches she'd made and took the hose and gently watered them down. She would have to get them into the garden pretty fast, but she wanted to wait until she saw what was being offered tomorrow, so she could plan out her garden a bit better.

The fact that there was a hydrangea, which could easily grow twelve feet, and it was a purple one from the looks of it, confirmed the need to plan. Heidi also had pink and white ones, so, if Doreen could manage to get a little piece of each, she could have all three as centerpieces, with a ton of other plants all around them.

Excited, delighted, and heartened by the kindness shown her by a stranger, while realizing just how much fun this would be, she gave the plants a really good soaking and then left them lightly covered in soil for the night so they wouldn't dry out, and headed inside. It wasn't dark, but it was getting dark, and she was happy to call it a day.

Inside she checked her emails. She clicked on one, seeing it was from Mack. He'd sent a file.

Or what appeared to be a screenshot of an old file. Excited, she realized it was a copy of the file from the robbery. As she sat down to read it, she found it incredibly sparse.

There had been an evening break-in. The door locks had been broken, and a window had been smashed. The robbery, it seemed, had been interrupted partway through. They had managed to get a certain amount of jewelry, then had suddenly taken off. Nobody had been caught, so no one had been tried or even charged for the crime.

Some of the jewels had been recovered at the scene. Some were on the ground, and some were dropped in a trail outside. It stopped where a vehicle had pulled up to the curb, and the robber had taken off. Was it just one robber or possibly two, given the amount of damage done and where it was located?

No suspects were ever charged. Also in the file was a note saying some of the items were insured, and some were not.

What she really needed now was a copy of the insurance policy. She emailed Mack back, asking if there was any way to get copies of the insurance files.

Mack responded quickly. **No, not unless you contact the company.**

That's what I thought. Thank you, Mack.

She opened up the file in a new search tab and saw Hobart's Insurance had been bought by West Liner and was still in business today. Together, Aretha and her husband had sold it.

He was now deceased, but she was living off the proceeds of the sale, and West Liner had been taken over by a much bigger insurance company, although they had kept the name. She went to their website and found that, as suspected, it was a fancy modern insurance company.

Already they wanted her to come in to get various quotes. And maybe that was something she should do, even on her own house. Now that all the antiques were gone, perhaps she could get a cheaper policy—if Nan had even insured the antiques in the first place, which was a legitimate question. Of course, that would just give Doreen more nightmares, thinking about the fact that something major could have happened, and all those wonderful antiques might have been lost.

Very quickly, she tired of the fussing and worrying and realized it was close to bedtime, and she began preparing to get there. Going up for a hot shower, it wasn't long before she crashed in bed and soon was out.

Chapter 11

Sunday Morning ...

DAWN BROKE BRIGHT, clear, and sunny. It would be another warm day. Doreen got up feeling sore from all the heavy digging the day before, then realized it was almost nine o'clock. She had to be down at Heidi's in an hour.

Shocked, she dressed, raced downstairs, then put on her faithful coffee and popped some bread in the toaster. She wondered about taking the animals as she fed them.

"Mugs, should I leave you here, or should I take you along?"

Since she was driving, she could take them all, but keeping track of them might prove to be a handful. She really wanted to get Goliath out in the car more, and a six-block trip wouldn't be too bad for him. At least she hoped not.

She headed outside, packing up a couple buckets she had and lots of bags. Garbage bags, so they would hold the roots.

She didn't know just how much she was bringing back but hoped it was a lot. It wasn't like her garden didn't need more. In fact, it needed a lot more.

She also needed to get that sod out from the side of the garden too because, if Mack was coming early, they could potentially start on the deck. And, with that, she grinned.

Toast eaten, pets fed, coffee—first cup down, second cup in a travel mug—she loaded everybody up and drove to her destination. As she arrived, the gates opened in front of her. She wasn't sure what to do, but Heidi was there motioning at her to come in. She drove in and parked off to the side, letting the animals out.

"I'm sorry. I never thought to ask," Doreen said, with a moment of regret, as the animals tumbled forward. "Is it okay that I brought them?"

Heidi laughed as she crouched to give Mugs a big greeting. Not to be left out, Goliath sauntered toward her too. She gave both a good scratching. "I'm absolutely delighted you brought them," she said. "Aretha is allergic, so I can't have pets."

"I'm sorry," Doreen said. "That's got to be really hard."

"It is," she said, "because I do like my animals."

"I don't know, Heidi. I think, for myself, even if I found I was allergic to just one of them, I don't know that I could get rid of these guys." Doreen gently patted Thaddeus, who sat on her shoulder.

"Of course not," she said. "That would be a travesty."

"Yep. That's kind of how I feel." Doreen shared a bright smile. "So, where are we starting?" Doreen opened the hatch of her car. "I brought some bags and buckets and my shovel."

"Perfect. I would start over in this bed." As Doreen walked with her, Heidi spoke of what she'd done that morning. "I've already pulled a bunch of plants for you, but feel free not to take something if you don't want it. I can always toss it into the compost bin."

"Maybe," Doreen said. "But, like you, I really hate to

not give each plant a chance at a good life."

"Oh my," Heidi said with a laugh. "Then you'll be taking home a lot of plants today."

They got started with the first bag. Heidi collected a half-dozen smaller plants, and then they got to the gladiolas, which she quickly and decisively split with a hard shovel and a boot, splicing off a great big group of brown, then yellow, then red glads.

"These are beautiful." Doreen admired them. "And they will grow nicely."

"That they will," Heidi said. "I have different colors on the other side, if you want more colors."

"Absolutely." Doreen quickly bagged those up and put them off to the side of her car. She popped the back seat down and stood the gladiolas up in the corner.

That's what they did for the next hour, walking through the garden, splitting off, dividing up, and taking out some of the volunteers crowding the garden. By the time they got one side of the garden done, Doreen's car was surprisingly full. It wasn't completely full yet, and she could certainly get a lot more in. But it was looking amazingly lush.

And the garden behind them was now looking much better as well, with lots more space between the plants as they raked and moved the bark mulch back and forth to leave the garden looking perfect in every spot. They started on the second side.

"This is a lot of plants," Heidi said with a laugh.

"As long as you're giving me only what you don't want," Doreen said, "then I'm happy to take them all."

"Not a problem," Heidi said.

And they kept working away.

By the time they were done, the car was more than full.

"Wow," Doreen said.

"There are still more outside the fence," Heidi smiled, "if you want some of those." She looked at the car doubtfully. "I'm not sure you have any room though."

"I can get more in," Doreen told her. Then she muttered to herself, "Of course who knows just how many it'll be?"

Outside the fence, they wandered along the beautiful phlox and another wandering plant, plus a whole pile of dianthus and carnations. Heidi cut and divided, even though the time of year wasn't necessarily perfect for pruning or transplanting. Doreen would take them home and give them all the love and care she possibly could.

By next year they would have had six months of growing time, depending on frost, and they would be doing so much better. By the time Doreen and Heidi had done the outside garden, her car was beyond stuffed. She sighed happily. "Thank you, thank you, thank you. It would have taken me a long time to buy or otherwise acquire this many plants."

"It's not a problem," Heidi said. "I'm just delighted I didn't have to kill all those wonderful plants."

"No," Doreen said. "I will be more than happy to put all these in my garden." Turning, she looked up at the house. "It's too bad Aretha doesn't like gardening."

"She doesn't like anything that gets her hands dirty," Heidi said. "We're as different as chalk and cheese."

"How did she end up coming to live with you?"

"Well, I'm not too proud to admit that I could use the money, and Aretha wasn't doing so well at Rosemoor. She was looking for something more private."

"So, she's like a boarder?"

Heidi nodded. "Yes. This is my home, and she stays here with me. It's nice to have the companionship, honestly," she said, "and she's a decent cook too. So it's kind of nice. Between the two of us, we manage quite well together."

"I'm delighted to hear that," Doreen said with a smile. "I'd hate to think of her being all alone and unhappy."

"Exactly," Heidi said. "And she doesn't have as much money as she wants everybody to believe. In fact, I don't think she has very much at all. But, as long as she's still paying me, I can keep the bills paid here."

"Is that why you're doing your own gardening?"

"My ability to keep the team of gardeners around is long gone," Heidi said. "Times have been tough, and my husband is long gone too. I diversified and made a few difficult judgment decisions on the investments that may not have done me any good. The fact of the matter is, Aretha filled a necessary void for me."

"There's nothing wrong with that," Doreen said.

"You don't have a job either, do you?" Heidi asked curiously, as she looked at the animals. "My understanding is that Nan gave you the house."

"She sure did," Doreen said with a laugh. "I inherited the ancient plumbing, the roof that needs fixing, and the antique furniture crammed from floor to ceiling."

"Oh, no." Heidi laughed. "Isn't that the truth? We get these theoretical gold mines, but it's up to us to figure out how to get through it all and how to turn the detritus into gold."

"Exactly," Doreen said. "But honestly, despite the challenges, I'm having a great time dealing with it."

"Perfect," Heidi said. "Anyway, if you ever want any more, just come on back and let me know."

"If you're ever dividing more, let me know."

"It sure looks great right now though." Heidi motioned

around.

"Thank you again, Heidi." Doreen walked over to the car, calling out to the animals.

Mugs came, and she had to rearrange things to fit him into the car because just so many plants were there now. But, with Mugs on the floor, Goliath on the seat, and Thaddeus on her shoulder, she finally had everything in the car.

At that, Heidi headed up to the front door. Doreen had gotten into the car and started it when Aretha was suddenly at her side.

"You stay away from here now," she said, leaning into the car.

Doreen settled back and looked up at the old woman. "Aretha, I'm sorry you're so unhappy," she said. "Heidi is a lovely person. Make sure you're nice enough to her that you get to stay here when your money runs out."

Instantly the woman stiffened, and she hissed, "I'm totally fine financially, and what do you know about it?"

"I know a lot more than you think," Doreen said sadly. "And I also know what it's like to have had money and then to find yourself without it. If you ever want to talk, you know where I live."

And, with that, she drove away, leaving the older woman standing with her jaw open. As she headed back home, she smiled. "Take *that*, universe. You don't have to lower yourself to being who everybody around you is or thinks you are."

As she drove in, she saw Mack's truck in the driveway and realized how late it was. Instead of pulling into the garage with the car so full, she just drove up beside him and parked. Mack wasn't in the truck. She let the animals out and started unloading the bags onto the driveway. Mugs hit the pavement and raced around back, woofing and woofing. She could hear Mack talking to him and suddenly he was here beside her, looking at her in surprise. She smiled and explained what happened.

"And this was Aretha?"

"No, it's where Aretha is staying. She's a boarder at Heidi's place."

"Oh," he said. "Heidi is a lovely lady."

"I know, and look at all the plants she gave me. I'm absolutely thrilled."

Mack looked at them in surprise and picked up the bags she had already unloaded. "I'll take these and come back."

She smiled up at him and, in a teasing voice, said, "Perfect timing. Who knew I would need your muscles?"

"Ha," he said. "I figured you did it on purpose."

"No," she said. "I forgot you were coming."

"Ouch," he winced. "That bites."

"Oops," she said to his retreating back. That wasn't very diplomatic of her.

She unloaded the rest, piling the bags all around her, and then, when she could, she closed the door. She grabbed a couple of the larger plants in the bags, just when he came back and snagged up all the rest.

"You're right. A lot is here," he said.

"There is. But, by the time I get them in the garden, it won't look like much. The garden needs to be replenished so much."

"I got a quote for you on the guy who brings in the topsoil bags too," he said. "One of my coworkers just had it done. It cost $110."

"I wonder how big the bag is?" she murmured.

"I think a pickup load size," he said. "Which we could

do instead. We could just dump it in front, if you want, or he might be able to swing it around and put it on the side."

"So it would be a bag by the garage maybe," she said.

He nodded. "I kind of like that idea myself. Then you could unload it as it's needed."

"I know. But, at the same time, it's $110." She wrinkled up her face at that.

"But you just got a whole pile of free plants," he pointed out. "And they need to be looked after, so they'll really need that quality soil."

"I know," she said.

"And, by the way," he dug his hand into his pocket, "I didn't pay you for doing Mom's garden." He handed her the forty dollars she'd come to expect.

She grinned at it. "You know, if I save this for three weeks …"

He nodded. "It would pay for one bag. Or we could just do the truckload."

"But how do we get it off your truck?"

He gave her an evil smile. "You shovel it."

She stared at him aghast. "Your truck doesn't just lift and dump?"

"Seriously?" He looked at her and chuckled.

She glared at him. "It would make sense, you know? Otherwise you have to fill it and then empty it."

"Not only fill and empty it"—he appeared as if he wasn't looking forward to the work—"you've got to wheel it all the way around to the back."

"You know what? That $110 isn't sounding too bad right now," she said a little more brightly.

"I figured you'd see it that way pretty quickly," he said.

"I wonder how long it would take."

"You could probably get it tomorrow. But I doubt you could get it today."

"Good point," she said. "But that is something we could do tomorrow."

"Not *we*," he said. "I've got to work. Remember?"

She raised her hands in surrender. "It was just a figure of speech. So maybe next week I'll get one then."

"*Uh-huh*," he said, as if not believing her.

She just glared at him. "Honest."

Now around in the backyard, she took one look at all the bags and plants.

"I really need to get these into the ground."

"I highly suggest you water the bags to keep them alive and maybe call in an order of topsoil first thing in the morning and get started. By the time you're done with one, then you can order another one."

She winced at that too. "I wonder if there's a price break for ordering in multiples."

"Maybe, but chances are you have to do a lot more than one or two," he said.

"Maybe. I don't know. I'm parking that idea for a bit." She walked around a little farther, studying the big gardens she still hadn't finished weeding and groaned. "This is where I'd like to have my team of gardeners because I've still got this to finish." She pointed at the garden where at least twelve feet back there still needed to be weeded before she could put new plants in, and then she looked at the deck. "Not to mention this to finish." When she realized that the one-quarter she had done was now well over half done, she looked at him in shock. "Did you do that?"

He nodded. "I was expecting you to be here, and, when you weren't, I just started working."

"Your mama trained you well," she said with a laugh.

"Unfortunately, yes," he said with a grin. "So tell me. Did you find out any more about the jewels?"

"Nothing except that, according to Nan, the business burned down. And our Aretha remarried after her husband's death. Oddly enough, she married the insurance guy who had insured her business. And, after they sold the insurance business to a much bigger insurance company, he passed on. This according to Nan and the internet."

"It's still interesting though," he said. "Is that pointing you in any direction?"

"Yeah, the husband," she said. "The first one. He appears to have been a complete mess and made bad business decisions."

"Do you think it was insurance fraud?"

"I don't know," she said, "but I want to talk to the company."

"Just because they bought the company doesn't mean they'll have the records. A lot of years have passed."

"I know," she said. "I suspect the answers I need are all in Aretha's head. But she's a very unhappy woman."

"And nobody else is left, is there?"

At that, she snapped her fingers. "Yes, there is," she said. "Mangus, that's her husband's brother. The second husband. He's having some procedure done this weekend, so I can't talk to him until Monday."

"Interesting," he said. "In other words, the case is still ongoing."

"Not only ongoing," she said, "I'm really wondering if those jewels are rightfully Aretha's or not."

"What will you do if they are?"

She shook her head. "I'm not sure. The woman definitely needs money. I just don't know how badly." She looked at Mack. "And your mother gave them to me. What do you want to do with the jewels?"

He shrugged. "They don't feel like mine," he said.

She smiled up at him. "I know what you mean," she said, "because they don't feel like they are mine either." She turned and looked at the dirt behind him. "You know what? I really need to get digging, don't I?"

"If you want a deck, you sure do," he said.

She groaned, then grabbed her digging fork. "Did you at least put on coffee?"

"No," he said. "You put the security system on, so I left it as is."

She looked up and smiled a genuine smile. "You're right," she said. "I almost forgot to do it when I left. But now that I have these jewels ..."

"Let's not forget you also have the other jewels."

"What other jewels?" She frowned up at him.

"The emerald necklace and earrings from your grand-mother, the pearls?"

Her face softened. "You're right," she said. "I'm really hoping not to have to sell those, but I guess I should get them appraised."

"You should," he said. "But maybe not from that same jeweler."

"No." She laughed. "I don't intend to go back there."

"Do you really think something was odd about that one appraiser?"

"Definitely something was odd about him and I don't know what to think about that Mindy person," she said. "But I just don't know how odd."

"What do you mean by that?"

"He didn't want to let the jewels go," she said slowly. "So I don't know if he recognized them somehow, but he wanted to buy them off me right then. Maybe he was just the kind of guy who saw something of good quality that then slipped through his fingers when I took them back, and he couldn't reconcile himself with the fact he couldn't have them."

"Do you think he's dangerous?"

She looked at him, smiled, and said, "Honestly, Mack, that's something you've been pounding into me since we first met. Everybody under the right circumstances is dangerous. If you're asking if this guy is dangerous to me, I'll have to say I believe he is."

As she said it, she realized inside it really was true. Something was off about that guy. He had really wanted those jewels, and that made him dangerous.

She just didn't know how bad it would get.

Chapter 12

Sunday Early Afternoon ...

IT WAS AMAZING how much work could be accomplished with the two of them working together. Doreen wasn't sure if Mack had planned to be here all afternoon helping her out, but he'd done so much already, and then he just put his shoulder to it and kept on working. And she, for one, really appreciated it.

"Thank you for all this," she murmured, looking at him.

"Not a problem. I wasn't planning on coming over quite so early," he muttered, as he dug the shovel yet again. "Considering we'll do dinner tonight."

"And I have an awful lot of gardening to do." Looking down at her watch, she groaned. "It's well past lunchtime too."

"Yeah. I didn't get here until twelve o'clock," he said, "And you were hours down with Heidi."

"More than I expected," she admitted. "It was nice to have somebody of a like mind and a shared hobby to visit with."

"Have you managed to make any friends since you moved in?"

"No," she said with a bite to her tone. "It seems like the only women I ever meet get embroiled in one of the cases, and they don't have the same view of me by the end of it all."

Mack laughed at that. "Can't really blame them," he said. "Look at Penny. You're putting her in jail for years."

"That is not my fault," Doreen said. "That woman attacked me."

"And that's not all she did," Mack said. He brought over the wheelbarrow and filled it with another load of compost material. "I'll take this out front."

She nodded and bent again, tossing in a few more clumps. "Do you think we'll get much farther on this?"

"You're getting a little bit done every time. I do need to go shopping, but that won't take long. I'll come back later for dinner."

"While you're gone," she said, "I'll eat some food. I only had toast for breakfast."

He stopped, turned, and glared at her.

She glared right back. "I did go shopping yesterday," she said. "So I can make a sandwich."

He rolled his eyes. "Are you eating anything other than sandwiches?"

"I made an omelet yesterday," she said. "I even added mushrooms."

A pleased smile played at the corner of his lips. "How about you do some more pasta?"

"I'd love to," she said. "I was thinking maybe you could cook some while you're here."

"How about I watch while you cook some?" he asked.

She gave a decisive nod. "That's probably better. Do you know I can't remember what we're supposed to have for dinner?" Worried, she chewed on her bottom lip. "Did we ever decide?"

"That's why I'm going shopping," he said. "We had talked about lamb chops, but I have a craving for salmon."

She stared at him. "Can we afford that?"

"I can," he said cheerfully. "So, if I pick up salmon for tonight, do you have any vegetables?"

She shrugged. "I have fresh vegetables for a salad. Nan sent them home with me."

"Any rice?"

"Still got that partial bag from when you cooked it last time."

"So how about we just keep it simple then. Salmon and a salad with some steamed rice."

"That works," she said. Then she looked at him again. "Or we could have pasta on the side."

He chuckled. "Or maybe we can cook pasta along with the salmon," he said.

"Sounds good," she said. "We could put the salmon *in* the pasta?"

He looked at her, frowning. "Like in a cream sauce with a bit of dill?"

Her face lit up. "Yes," she said. "Fettuccine with a salmon dill sauce. Yum." She rubbed her hands together.

He chuckled. "We'll see. Listen. I'll take this out front and dump it. Then I'll leave you for a couple hours. I'll come back at five o'clock this afternoon."

Doreen checked her watch and said, "It's three already."

"I know," he said. "That's why I've got to go. Oh, somebody could be coming along with more materials for the deck."

She beamed. "Now that would be huge."

"It could be huge," he said. "I don't know that it's very much though. We'll have to see."

"Good enough," she said. She watched as he disappeared with the wheelbarrow, hoping he would bring it back, knowing she had to get the bulk of this done before he got home.

She worked away for the next hour until her growling stomach couldn't be ignored anymore. With the wheelbarrow full yet again, she took it out front to the compost bin, which was pretty darn full now. It would sink a little bit over time, but it was heaped. She would have to make a pile somewhere, then load it in the bin after it was emptied on Monday.

With that in mind, she headed back inside. The animals followed, going into the cooler house, where she scrubbed her hands and face free of dirt, and then sat down to make a sandwich. Being so hungry, she made two big ones and then cut them in half and sat outside on the small deck. Thaddeus sat beside her, munching away on little bits of greens she had put out for him. She had brought treats for Mugs and Goliath, not wanting to give them parts of her sandwich, which just went to show how hungry she was.

As she sat here, her phone rang. She looked down and didn't recognize the number. She answered, "Hello."

"Doreen," a man said with a far too cheerful outlook.

"Yes, who is this?"

"I understand you have some jewels you want appraised," the man said.

Her back stiffened. "I'm sorry. I don't know who you are. You must be mistaken. I don't know anything about any jewels."

"Did you find jewels in a little jewelry bag from Johnson

and Abelman?" the man asked, his tone turning harsh.

Doreen tried to listen intently, wondering who it was and whether it was the same man she'd met at the jewelry store. "I don't have a clue what you're talking about. Do you always phone strangers and talk about things like that?"

"I heard you have some jewels to be appraised."

"You don't know anything about it," she said calmly, then looked down at the number and knew she needed to write it down for Mack. She got up from her table and walked inside. "And please don't bother me again."

"I'm not trying to bother you," he said, "but those jewels are worth a lot of money. I'm quite prepared to pay handsomely for them."

"You haven't even seen them," she said. "So you have no idea of their value or just what sort of handsome price I might ask." She could feel her temper stirring, but she wrote down the number so she could trace it later. Or rather so Mack could.

"Well, keep my number handy," he said. "I have money, and I'm happy to pay for them. Quality is hard to find."

"I don't know what you're talking about."

"You've already admitted you do," he said, laughing. "Like I said, give me a call. They are worth a lot of money. You can feed yourself for a good long time on it."

"I don't have your name," she said, "and I don't deal with people who can't give me a name."

"Zachary," he said. "Zachary Winters." And, with that, he hung up.

She wrote down the name, along with the number, all thoughts of her sandwich having fled her mind.

"Now, who was he, and what relationship does he have to that jewelry store?" she asked, addressing no one in particular. Her mind was on her failed attempt to get an appraisal. Nobody else would know the quality of these jewels. Unless of course—she stopped in her tracks and looked down at the name. "Unless of course you had something to do with them going missing in the first place."

Chapter 13

Sunday Late Afternoon ...

HOURS LATER, DOREEN stopped digging when she heard a vehicle drive up her driveway. She looked at Mugs. "Sure hope that's Mack," she said. Mugs started barking and racing around to the side of the house. She dug the fork into the ground, picked up the wheelbarrow by its handles, and pushed it steadily out front. She got there just in time to see Mack hopping out with bags of groceries in his hands.

She smiled. "Before you take that in, any chance you can give this compost bin a good hard shake and see if I can pack more in? I've already started a pile for after it's emptied, but I'd love to add this in too."

He nodded and set the bags on the hood of his truck, then gave it a shake before pressing it all down farther. Afterward he gave her a hand moving the wheelbarrow contents into the bin. "You can probably get one more wheelbarrow load in," he said. "Then you're done."

"Good enough," she said. "I'll take this to the backyard. Thank you."

"You're welcome," he said. "I'll take these groceries in

and wash up."

"Sounds good," she said. "I'm tired and hungry."

"Good because I never got that coffee earlier, and I really could use a cup."

"Me too. I'll put it on in a minute," she called back, laughing. The coffee was killing her in price, but it was such a nice social thing between the two of them that she didn't want it to stop. She wouldn't be at all surprised if he came here just for the coffee.

She returned to her backyard and picked up the rest of the sod and noted she was almost there. If she was lucky, they could get it all into the compost bin. If not, she'd fill the wheelbarrow and leave it until the compost was dumped, rather than making the pile out front any bigger.

She worked steadily until she heard the door bang and looked up to see Mack with two cups of coffee in his hands. He walked down the steps, surveyed the area, and said, "Wow, you got a lot more done than I thought."

"It's so uneven though," she said. "I hope that won't be a problem."

"We'll have to level off the blocks anyway," he said.

She straightened up after shaking the last dirt off the sod, throwing it into the wheelbarrow. "There. I'm done." She smiled and accepted the coffee. "It's great to have the physical accomplishment, but I will be sore tomorrow."

Mack looked around at the bag still full of plants. "Don't you need to get those into the ground today?"

"I should," she said. "They're already wilting. But I'm not sure where I want to put them all."

"Isn't it better to get them in and save them, knowing you can move them later?"

"Maybe," she said. With coffees in hand, they wandered

up and down her backyard, looking at places where she would put things.

"Why don't you hold my cup, and we'll just start planting." Grabbing the shovel, Mack said, "What was it you were just saying? You wanted to put something where?"

She pointed out where she wanted the gladiolas. "They need a lot of space because they'll multiply quickly, but I thought we'd put a clump in the center of each of these fence panels." She was pointing from the creek back toward her house. She had ten panels of fence, and only three clumps of glads, but she knew Millicent had big clumps of blue ones, which Doreen hoped to get corms from.

Mack grabbed the bags with the gladiolas, and, before long, they were in place.

Doreen had some bone meal and a little natural fertilizer, so she put that in too. "The ground is decent here, and these things tend to grow anywhere anyway." A few weeds were stuck in between them, so she carefully pulled them out.

They got into a routine, and, while Mack dug more holes, Doreen was busy planting. And, just like that, the gladiolas were in. She laughed. "I guess when there's two of us, a lot of work can get done."

"A lot of people like to think about things first," he said. "I tend to be the kind of person who dives in and gets it done. You can always move things around later, after you see how it goes and what you like where."

"Good point," she said. "In the meantime, this was a huge help, and they all should survive."

They kept working until she straightened up and announced, "I think there's only one bag left."

"Figure out where you want to put them," he said. "I'll

get more coffee. Then we'll get them planted. After that, we'll see if we can get some soaker hoses going. Didn't you say Nan had a bunch?"

"I've got some in use already, but, yes, all of these need watering." Doreen watched as Mack picked up the two cups and headed back inside to finish the pot of coffee. She walked over to get the last bag, the collection of daisies in all colors. *A big center bed would be lovely*, she thought, as she walked through the garden. She noted the fifth and sixth fence panels really didn't have a whole lot, but the fifth was more visible to the middle of the yard because the tenth panel was up against the house and felt more like it was part of the house. She laid them all out so they each had a large space and put the painted daisies in front, as they would never grow as big or as lush as the others.

Now with everything laid out the way she wanted, she cleaned up all the bags, put them in the garbage, and accepted the cup of coffee from Mack when he came back out.

"Aren't very many left," she said, motioning toward the garden.

"Good enough," he said.

Just ten minutes later, everything was planted. As Doreen held Mack's cup, he grabbed the soaker hoses, and, with her guidance, he gently laid them through the garden until they reached the back toward the creek. "The creek's pretty high," he commented.

"It's up now, but it's been going up and down in this six- to ten-inch range."

He nodded. "It makes sense, depending on the amount of melted snow coming down off the mountains and how many of the other rivers are drifting into your little creek.

The amounts will go up and down on a regular basis."

"It sure is beautiful though."

"It really is," he admitted. "This is quite a special property."

"That's what I thought. And here we are, finally getting it fixed up," she said. "I know the deck will make a huge difference when it comes to enjoying the backyard property."

"Yes," he said, "and for adding to your living space."

"Exactly."

With one final look at the creek, Doreen turned toward the garden. "I want to get these watered, now that everything's in." She walked back and turned on the hose, then watched as it seeped through the ground.

"You might want to grab a hose and spray some of these down," Mack suggested.

She nodded and was already set up for it with the proper fittings. She just needed to screw on the second hose and grab a nozzle. Then she walked up and down the garden. Unfortunately it only reached partway, so she had to raise the stream, shooting it back as far as it could go. She was able to soak the new transplants, which was the only real goal for watering tonight. Turning that hose off, she left the soakers running, then looked at Mack with a weary smile. "Can we eat now?"

He burst out laughing. "Maybe. Pretty tired, huh?"

"I am," she said. "And it's definitely food time."

"Did you get sandwiches earlier?"

"I did," she said, "but got interrupted, and it wasn't enough."

He smiled with a nod. "Okay. Let's go get some food."

Cheerfully, Doreen headed up the small deck and looked down at the large area they had cleared. "Wow, we're actually getting somewhere."

"Speaking of which," Mack said, "did anybody deliver more deck supplies?"

"No. Not that I saw."

"That's fine. Maybe he couldn't come today." He walked inside, and, as Doreen watched, Mack put on the water for the pasta she was so desperate to have. Then he opened the fridge and took out a beautiful slab of salmon.

She gasped with joy. "That looks so wonderful," she said.

"We'll precook it slightly in the cream sauce, and then add it to the pasta."

Doreen nodded, set up her phone to Record, but she also watched his every move.

While they waited for the pasta to boil, Mack turned on another burner on the stove and sautéed the salmon until it was just about ready. Making sure no bones were inside, he removed the skin and then started the sauce in the pan where the salmon had been cooking. Very quickly he had a nice cream sauce, and he gently laid in the salmon.

"You can put this sauce onto the salmon, then put the pasta on top, or put the sauce on the pasta and put the salmon on top of the sauce. But this way is just as easy too." He stirred it lightly, and the dill aroma came through.

"Wow," she said. "It smells marvelous."

Mack looked at her seriously. "I'm doing my part. How about you? Is the salad done?"

"Oops." Doreen's cheeks turned a bit pink, and she ran to get out the salad fixings. As she washed the lettuce, she said, "Oh, by the way, I got a really weird phone call while you were gone." She proceeded to tell him about it.

"Zachary Winters," he said, frowning.

"Yeah, I don't know him, but he was trying to buy those jewels from me."

"How do you think he found out about them?"

"My first thought is the jewelry store," she said, "but I don't have any basis for that."

"Makes sense to me. I guess there's no such thing as expectation of privacy on a deal like that."

"Well, there should have been," she said, frowning. "Jewelry stores need to be attentive to such matters because most of their clients have money. Obviously you don't want to set up your clients for robberies."

"I don't know the name," Mack said frowning. "Then it's not an industry where I know any of the players."

"I've got his number," Doreen said. "He told me to make sure I had his number, in case I wanted to sell the jewelry. I was also thinking," she continued, "that maybe he had something to do with the jewel theft, or at least knew about them, because, outside of the people at the jewelry store, who else would have known?"

"I don't know," Mack said. "When you think about it, the jewels were turned in to the police. So there could be all kinds of people from there who knew. And they could have mentioned them to others."

"That's true. Maybe your mom was asked to sell them when she turned them in."

"No clue. Maybe we should find out." While the pasta boiled, and Mack kept an eye on the sauce, he called his mother.

Doreen listened to his conversation with Millicent but only heard half of it.

When he hung up, he turned to Doreen and said, "She doesn't remember much. At the time she thought several people had offered to buy them. But she wasn't interested in selling because she didn't consider them as belonging to her and my dad."

"So how long do you think she had the house before she found the jewels?"

He shook his head. "Not too long. Not long at all."

Chapter 14

Sunday Dinnertime …

"BUT," MACK SAID. "There are pictures of the old house, way back before they bought it, and that juniper was encroaching the driveway badly. It was pretty big already."

"Interesting," Doreen said. "I wonder how long the jewels were there? Maybe they were buried in a rush with the intention of moving them later?"

"I don't know. The velvet bag wasn't superdeep into the tree, according to Mom. They found it when they were trying to get the roots out."

"But why, if somebody hid it there, wouldn't they have come back?"

"The most likely reason is they couldn't."

As soon as the salad was done, Doreen watched Mack drain the pasta, coat it with butter, and then served some on their plates. All the while her stomach grumbled. He gently scooped the salmon and dill sauce over the top. She stared at it in amazement. "You did that so easily," she breathed.

"It is easy," he said, as he put the pan back on the stove.

She was delighted to see there would be leftovers. He'd

served himself a larger portion than hers, but she was okay with that because hers was still huge. And he'd done a lot of physical work today too. He carried both plates as she led the way, racing in front to let him out the kitchen door to the deck table. She quickly came back with the salad and cutlery. As they sat down, she marveled. "Whoever would have thought you could make something like this?"

He chuckled and said, "There are lots of leftovers."

"Which is a good thing," she said. "Now I can eat for the week."

Mack just shook his head at that.

When Doreen bit in and tasted it, she moaned in joy. "Did you add lemon juice when I wasn't looking?" she asked suspiciously.

"You videoed when I made the sauce."

"But you sent me off to make salad," she said. "So I don't know what I might have missed out on."

"It's not hard," he said. "You saw me make it."

"I still haven't cooked pasta on my own yet," she admitted.

"You were supposed to do that from start to finish tonight," he said with a crestfallen look.

"You'll just have to come back and cook more," she said.

"Next time I come, you're cooking. Somehow this went from me teaching you to cook, to me cooking and you eating."

"That works too," she said with a cheerful grin.

He rolled his eyes at her, and the two dug in.

By the time Doreen's plate was empty, her stomach thought it had died and gone to heaven. "This is absolutely wonderful," she said for the umpteenth time, as she scooped up the last of the sauce on her plate.

"There is more, if you want it," Mack said.

She settled against her chairback. "I don't think I can eat another bite. I'm pretty full."

"Good," he said. "Then you have leftovers for at least tomorrow night, if not more."

As she thought back to the amount of sauce in the pan, she nodded. "At least two nights," she said, "and probably more noodles than that."

"But you can eat the noodles plain."

"Or fried with eggs," she said enthusiastically.

"Or just with cheese," he said.

She nodded. "Leftover noodles are never wrong here," she said with a laugh.

Just then a banging at the front door reverberated throughout the house. Mugs barked. Mack looked at her, surprised. Doreen shrugged. "I'm not expecting anyone."

"Ah," he said, "but I am. It could be the guy from work." Together they walked to the front door, and Doreen opened it. Standing there was a man she vaguely remembered seeing at crime scenes. The two men greeted each other.

Mack's coworker looked at him. "I wasn't expecting to see you here."

"I've been working in the garden all afternoon," Mack said with a groan. "Canton, Doreen. Doreen, Canton."

The guy laughed. "Well, give me a hand unloading this, will you?"

The three headed to his truck full of a pile of boards and what looked like steel posts. Doreen wasn't sure what those would be used for, but Mack was pretty happy to see it all. She helped carry the other stuff, which were weird little shapes with big screws on them, as well as other kinds of hardware, including boxes of screws. This was the deck hardware Mack had been talking about. She carried as much of it back as she could. Not wanting to leave the boxes of hardware outside, she put them in the kitchen on the table. By the time the guy left, she had her list of supplies out, trying to figure out what they had just been given.

Together, standing at the kitchen table with the back door wide open, the two marked off everything they had collected today and reassessed the list. Mack looked at it, nodded, and said, "You're down to only needing about four or five hundred dollars now."

"Seriously?"

He nodded. "There's a good chance, yes. Next week's a long weekend for me with my schedule. You may want to consider getting a start on it then."

Doreen looked at the grass and sod she had moved. "And here I thought we already had started."

Mack chuckled. "It's too big of a job to start leveling off the foundation blocks now. Considering it's late Sunday evening and all. But maybe Friday we can start getting those in."

"You'll need some help though, won't you?" she asked.

He shrugged. "If there isn't any help, there isn't any help. That just means it'll take a bit longer."

She nodded. "It would be nice to have help. I don't know if I can help carry much of this heavier stuff."

"Don't worry about it," he said. "I might see if anybody is available."

"I doubt if too many people will want to come help me," she said in a dry tone. "I'm pretty sure I've used up all my goodwill at the police force."

"Nope, not at all," he said. "They might not like all the

extra work, but they like closing cases and bringing whatever closure we can to the families. So that's not an issue."

Doreen smiled. "That would be great," she said. "And who knows? Maybe this week I'll solve another case."

Mack rolled his eyes at her and groaned. "How about this week you just stay out of trouble?"

"I'm never in trouble," she protested.

"And don't contact this Zachary guy," he said. "I want to see who he is first."

"As soon as you leave tonight," she said cheerfully, "I'll research him myself."

"Send me whatever you find. Obviously the jewels are worth a lot of money, maybe even more than you expected."

"Maybe. But a part of me feels like the mystery surrounding them is the bigger part of this."

"I don't think any deaths were associated with the crimes back then," he said. "And white-collar crimes on a case so cold as this? It will be really hard to find enough evidence to bring charges."

"Unless somebody confesses," she said.

"True enough." Mack tilted his head. "And, for whatever reason, people tend to open their mouths and tell you all kinds of stuff."

"Too bad I couldn't get Aretha to talk to me." Doreen brightened. "But tomorrow is a new day, and I'll go talk to Mangus."

"Keep me informed," he said, then walked his cup to the sink. "I'm gonna head home." Looking at the mess, he frowned. "But I should help you with these dishes first."

She shook her head. "Go on home. You did enough work today."

When he glanced at her suspiciously, she gave him a

bland smile.

"What are you up to?"

"Nothing." Inside she was itching to figure out who Zachary Winters was. "Besides, there are hardly any dishes to wash." Doreen carried their plates in from outside, while Mack hesitated. "Go on," she said gently. "I'm more than grateful that you cooked, not to mention all the outside work."

"Fine," he said. "Have a good night."

"Yes, I will." She walked with him to the front door. As he stepped out, she said, "What about your two old lady deaths? Are you about to find out any more about them?"

"Waiting on the autopsy reports," he said. "So far we can't tell if they're suspicious. Remember? We get called in for any unusual death."

"Makes sense, particularly if they're older," she said.

"We all die sometime," he said, and, with a small wave, he walked to his truck and hopped in. With all the animals at her feet, Doreen watched as he drove down the cul-de-sac and took off.

Chapter 15

Monday Morning ...

MONDAY MORNING DOREEN hopped out of bed and had her shower, happy to ignore the aches and pains from the heavy gardening yesterday, as she realized how much closer they were to getting the deck started. And, with the added contributions yesterday, she was seriously thrilled.

As she headed downstairs, thinking about breakfast, her mind immediately went to her dinner leftovers. She winced. "I certainly can't have dinner right now," she muttered to herself. She put on her coffee, opened her fridge, and saw the pasta. Determinedly she shut the fridge, put several pieces of bread in the toaster, and had peanut butter and jam with a chunk of cheese on the side. If nothing else, she would have this for breakfast and save the pasta for lunch. As soon as it was nine o'clock, she dialed Nan.

"Good morning, dear. How are you?" Nan said in her gentle voice, a reminder of all Doreen had missed during those years when she had been so unhappily married.

She smiled. "I'm good. I had a good night's sleep. I was wondering if it would be a good time to come and talk to Mangus."

"Most likely," Nan said. "We'll be leaving for lawn bowling practice in an hour, so he'll be eating and then getting ready."

"Could you contact him?" Doreen asked cautiously. "Just to see if he'd even be willing to talk to me?"

"I can do that. Let me call you back." Nan hung up. By then the coffee had dripped. Doreen had had one cup when Nan called back. "He's just about to sit outside for tea in the garden and wants to know if you'll join him."

Doreen glanced down at her coffee. "Yes, of course I will."

"Good," Nan said. "Come to my place, and we'll both head out."

"Perfect," Doreen said with a laugh. She hopped to her feet, added a dash of cold water to the little bit of space in her coffee cup, then guzzled down the coffee. The last thing she wanted was a caffeine headache. She had no intention of examining why she continued to drink something guaranteed to give her a headache if she didn't have enough.

Juggling the refilled cup and a bottle of water in one hand and the toast in her other hand, she walked to the creek, still eating. The animals were happy to be out and about, with Goliath racing ahead and then stopping until they passed him, then racing ahead again. Mugs just seemed to trot along quite happily. Thaddeus even kept up a rambling conversation the whole time. Basically he had been telling her how he was there for at least two minutes solid. When he finally ran out of steam, she reached up, gently caressed his forehead, the back of his head, and whispered to him, "Thaddeus is gorgeous."

He burst into his lovely little trill, calling out, repeating it over and over.

Doreen was still laughing as she stepped around the corner and headed toward Rosemoor Manor. Nan was waiting, watching Thaddeus in astonishment as he continued to trill, "Thaddeus is gorgeous," all the way toward Nan. She reached out a hand, and he hopped on, then made his way up to her shoulder. There he crooned against her cheek and rubbed his head gently back and forth.

Nan looked at Doreen in surprise.

Doreen laughed. "I don't know when he started that. I heard it the first time yesterday. And now, of course, he loves to say it."

"And, of course, he does it so well." Nan laughed. She gently hugged the little guy as she reached to pet Mugs and Goliath. "I hope you're hungry. Mangus has apparently chosen to have breakfast out there too."

Doreen's stomach growled, even though she'd already eaten.

Smiling at the sound, Nan said, "Good. Let's go have a feast."

Doreen groaned. "What if I've already eaten?"

"You'll eat again then," she said. "I'm sure it won't be a problem." Chuckling, Nan led the way. Out in the back garden, they stopped to make sure all the animals were following, and Doreen suddenly worried that she hadn't asked Nan about bringing them. She stepped behind Nan as they went around the building to the back, where a series of gardens and large tables with umbrellas were set up.

Doreen gasped. "Nan, what a beautiful backyard."

"It is, indeed," Nan said. "We often sit out here for tea and treats." She led the way past a small patio to where trees shaded the far corner. An older man sat there, his hand on his cane as he surveyed the table of goodies.

Doreen was astonished. "There's food here for six, if not more."

"I told him that you're hungry," Nan said in a whisper. "And remember. We don't have to pay extra for it here."

Doreen nodded. She watched as Nan called out to Mangus.

He lifted his head, then looked at her and smiled. "There you two are. Pardon, if I don't stand."

Doreen rushed over, reaching out to shake his hand. "Please don't get up. How kind of you to invite me for tea."

He motioned to the chair beside him. "It's always nice to have two lovely ladies join me for a meal," he said. "Of course, it might not be the healthiest of meals, but it's definitely my first choice when it comes to food nowadays."

Doreen looked at the selection of doughnuts and cinnamon buns with some nut breads and croissants. "Looks wonderful," she admitted. "I'm sure the Rosemoor dietitians won't agree with us though."

He chuckled. "At my age, I don't care what I eat anymore. Most things have shut down already anyway. Pretty soon they'll be putting this stuff in a blender and feeding it directly into my stomach." He shook his head. "And I won't have any of this." He looked at Nan. "And how are you doing, my dear?"

Nan blushed and smiled, almost coquettishly. Doreen watched in amazement as the two flirted. Apparently age had nothing to do with the confusing interactions between man and woman.

When they were done, Mangus turned to Doreen and pointed at the plates. "Please, help yourself and take several."

Doreen smiled; he was waiting for her to serve herself before he got something. She picked up a croissant and put it on her plate and then a cinnamon bun.

"A girl after my own heart," Mangus said, as he took a cinnamon bun and croissant as well. Then he frowned. "Oh, no cheese is here." Pulling out his phone, he sent a text.

Doreen watched in amazement as very quickly somebody from inside the manor came out, carrying a large plate.

The attendant smiled at the three of them. "You should have asked for the cheese in the first place."

"I know," Mangus said with a shrug. "You know what my memory is like."

The plate of cheese was put down in front of them, and a second plate with assorted jams, peanut butters, and honeys was added.

Doreen smiled. "This is just lovely. Thank you," she said warmly to the young woman.

Her name tag was on her shoulder, but Doreen couldn't read what it said. The woman just gave a small wave and walked away.

Doreen looked at Mangus. "You're lucky to be able to do this."

"I don't know how much luck has to do with it," he said. "We pay enough, don't we, Nan?"

Nan nodded. "Don't we ever," she said.

Doreen immediately wondered if Nan was still okay financially. She tossed her grandmother a worried frown.

But Nan just reached across the table and patted her hand. "My granddaughter is always concerned I'll run out of money," Nan said to Mangus.

He smiled and said, "Then you're very blessed."

The conversation died down as everybody dug in. And even though Doreen had already had two pieces of toast, she was no fool. She wouldn't need lunch after this, and she had lots of leftovers for dinner tonight. These were treats, too expensive to spend money on for herself, and she only ever got them when she came to see Nan.

With the croissant and cheese done, she cut the cinnamon bun into smaller pieces, as Nan lifted the teapot and poured tea for everyone.

"It's beautiful out here," Doreen said again, as a gentle breeze wafted through the backyard, letting the branches above them sway gently.

"It really is," Mangus said. "I prefer to sit out here when I have to sit anywhere."

She nodded. "I understand completely."

Mangus finished the cinnamon bun on his plate and reached for a doughnut and what looked like a slice of banana bread. Doreen smiled as he had no problem with taking two more of the treats. He motioned at her plate. "Eat up. Eat up."

She still had a bit of cinnamon bun left on her plate but reached for a piece of banana bread, setting it on her plate also.

With a note of satisfaction, Mangus nodded and sat back. "Now, why were you asking about Aretha?"

"Well, I don't want to spread this around, as I'm already getting suspicious phone calls, but I'm trying to find the owners of some jewels."

"Loose gems?" And he leaned forward and looked at her intently. "Now I have some questions for you."

Chapter 16

Monday Midmorning ...

AND WHEN MANGUS asked Doreen questions, she knew his mind was just as sharp as it had ever been. He wanted to know what kind of cuts, how many carats, what kind of stones, how many there were, where she'd found them, and why she was asking about his sister-in-law. When she had answered all she could, he nodded.

"Aretha is a bit of a sad case," he said. "She's still clinging to the glory days of old, but, in truth, she's living off her small pension and the little bit left from her husband, but she's not doing very well at all."

"I did see her at the home where she is staying," Doreen let him know.

"She's a boarder there," he clarified. "She wanted to stay here, but she doesn't have the funds." He hesitated, then continued, "I have to admit a part of me said I should help her out, but honestly I don't have that much more either. Particularly since they keep raising the rates here." He looked over at Nan, who agreed. "It is a problem. If I was dead already, then it wouldn't be such an issue, and she could have some of the money I have left, but I also have a family

I'm trying to help out."

"Of course." Doreen thought about the woman who had stood so proudly, actively mocking others. "She does appear to be stuck in a time warp."

"She can't possibly lose face and have everybody know she's as broke as she is, and she's not anywhere close to death's door," Mangus said. "She was married to my younger brother for many years. Selling that business was the best thing he could have done. At least that gave them some money."

"It should have given them a lot of money," Doreen said, wondering out loud. "Wouldn't it?"

"Maybe, but, when my brother died, he gave my nephews a big chunk of it. Aretha got some, but she had come into his life later, and he already had two sons, so both the boys needed an inheritance too."

"Had he done something with his money after the sale?" Doreen asked.

Mangus snorted. "You mean, besides bad investments? They had a custom motor home to travel in, and then they had an accident with that. Although there was some insurance, it didn't fix the problems they needed it to, so they lost money when they tried to sell it." He shook his head. "But that was my brother. Hobart was never the smartest or the brightest."

"Were they happy at least?" Doreen asked. It was terrible to think this woman had gone through such a series of setbacks.

"No, I don't think they were. My brother had married his childhood sweetheart, and, when she died of breast cancer, leaving him with two kids, I think he was desperate to have companionship, even if it wasn't the same as what he'd had before. It seemed to me that she was looking for someone to look after her. My brother probably looked like a great deal, perhaps because of the insurance company. You might assume there would be bad blood between them because of the prior coverage problems, but instead the incident appears to have given them something to bond around. But the fact of the matter is, when my brother died, not a whole lot of money was left. It's been quite a few years now, so I'm sure she's got very little left."

"Heidi appeared to be a lovely lady," Doreen said, and Mangus nodded.

"Oh, yes, she definitely is. She and I spoke about moving Aretha in there with her because, at the time, Heidi wasn't sure she wanted a *live-in companion*, so to speak. But she finally came around, realizing it was something she could do. Her father had been a minister and had helped out an awful lot of the community at various times, so Heidi felt maybe this was something she could do to help out too."

Aretha was a charity case, and that bothered Doreen tremendously. "I'm sorry for Aretha. That must have been a very hard change of circumstances."

"The burglary got them in trouble," Mangus said. "Her first husband was just a waste. He was terrible. I was good friends with her parents, and they were beside themselves as they tried to straighten out one mess after another, thanks to him. But that burglary?" He shook his head.

"And nobody ever figured out who did it, did they?"

"No," he said. "It was pretty darn sad, if you ask me."

"What I don't understand," Nan interjected, "is why the insurance didn't cover it all."

"Because, according to the jewelry store, they had just taken receipt of a large number of gems, and the cost of those gems wasn't covered under the insurance."

"But surely if they had receipts for it—"

"That was the problem. What most people don't know is …" He took a deep breath, as if warming up for a good story. "If my memory serves me correctly, there was an order for gems, and it was paid for, but then Reginald, Aretha's first husband, had called and added on to the order in a big way. He said he paid but couldn't prove it as he had no receipts. Remember. It wasn't the digital age back then, and nothing happened quickly. He said he'd paid. The seller said he hadn't. Against the seller's policy, I might add, the order was shipped out, but there was no paperwork with it. Or the paperwork disappeared." Mangus shook his head.

"Apparently, *according to Reginald*, what arrived didn't match what was ordered. While that was in a state of chaos, the break-in occurred, so they couldn't say exactly what was stolen, as they had no receipts and no appraisals for the new jewels. So, when the insurance paid out, it was only enough to cover the cost of the documented main order, without the new jewels added on. The insurance investigation checked with the supply house. It had receipts for what they shipped on the main order, but the add-ons that were phoned in didn't match what had been shipped. And then, with the insurance claim still unsettled and suspicious, soon afterward the big fire at Johnson and Abelman Jewelers burned up everything."

"So, it was a double insurance claim, is that it?" Doreen asked. "Oh, no, the insurance company dropped all coverage until this claim was settled, as they were suspicious of the theft claim—right?"

"Exactly. When the insurance investigator went to the store, they found the jewelry store didn't have the proper security or the updated fire alarms which the insurance company demanded, invalidating any coverage. So they got cold feet and dropped all coverage while they were still fighting over the insurance claim on the stolen jewels. Right before the fire happened."

"This was your brother's insurance company?"

"Yes, but he was only a part owner," Mangus said. "His silent partner—I forget his name now, but he passed on many years ago—was trying to keep the business afloat after that, and, of course, they wouldn't pay for anything they didn't have to."

"Which would also explain how he and Aretha bonded," Doreen said with a nod. "Because he would have blamed his partner for being the difficult one."

"Exactly," Mangus said. "But the truth of the matter is, my brother was very much a hard businessman anyway. And he made good money, but I know that both of his sons ended up in a lot of financial trouble, and he bailed them out. They were part of his first marriage to the wife he adored, so he did anything he could to make their lives easier. And, of course, he was married to Aretha back then, but he took care of his two sons first. I don't think he funneled much money into Aretha's pockets."

Doreen sat back as she worked away on the banana bread. She was surprised she could still eat so much, but it was so good. "Sounds like a very tragic life for Aretha."

"The trouble is, it's so hard to feel sorry for her," Nan said, "because she's not a very nice person."

"Particularly where women are concerned," Mangus added. "I think she's always seen women as competition. As her circumstances changed, she couldn't keep up."

"What about all the women who surround her?"

"That's a good question," Mangus said. "I'm not sure. Maybe it's still because she's one of the older families here, and that's why they like to hang around with her. Honestly, I'm happy if she does have some friends because she surely needs some." He frowned as he studied his plate. "So, what should I have next?"

Nan chuckled. "You haven't had any of this." She shoved what looked like small doughnuts toward him.

He reached out his fingers, hesitating over a couple of them, as if he couldn't choose. "Oh, what the heck," he said with a shrug, then picked up both. Doreen smiled. He caught the look on her face and grinned. "Hey, when you get to my age, nothing else matters." And then he looked at Doreen, reached to the same plate, picked up two more, and dumped them on her plate. "You are a big strapping girl," he said. "You can eat more too!"

Doreen stared in horror at the two sugary doughnuts, then chuckled. "I'll *be* a big strapping girl if I keep eating like this."

At that, he gave a loud guffaw of laughter. "You're a long way away from hitting that stage," he said. "In fact, you could use a few pounds."

She just rolled her eyes at that. "I had salmon with fettuccine in a creamy dill sauce last night. I'm hardly starving."

Nan, her eyes suddenly alight with curiosity, leaned forward. "Did Mack cook that for you?"

"Yes, and, while I saw what he did, or at least most of what he did, I'm still not sure I could ever replicate it."

"Who knew our detective would be such a good cook?" Mangus said.

"Not me," Doreen replied, "but I'm definitely reaping the benefits." She looked back at Mangus. "Did you ever have any theories about what happened with that break-in?"

"Sure did," he said. "I was pretty darn certain Reginald had orchestrated it."

Doreen sat back. "What an interesting theory," she said. "Why would you think that?"

"I suppose it comes from what I've heard from Aretha and her parents over the years. Her husband didn't have a lick of business sense, but he was also a bit of a buffoon. He wouldn't listen to advice from anyone. Every project he tried to manage blew up into a disaster. He just couldn't seem to get into the rhythm of what *business* meant. He had all these big schemes, one of which was to sell everything and then go buy all the lottery tickets he could, saying, *No way I can't win.*"

"Ouch," Nan said. "Sure they're rigged, but that just means it's even more rigged as you buy more. Plus back then lottery was a newish game in town. Nothing secure there."

Mangus nodded. "We all know that, but he was always looking for a get-rich-quick scheme."

"But he was a partner in a big jewelry company that would come down to him and his wife anyway," Doreen argued. "Why would he be in such a rush to become wealthy?"

"Because he didn't really want to work for a living," Mangus said. "Not like we did in the old days." He glanced at Nan, who was busy nodding in agreement as she ate some pastry Doreen honestly didn't remember seeing on the plates.

Doreen studied the plates to see if there were any more, then realized how ridiculous she was being because her plate still had a little piece of cinnamon bun, banana bread, and two sugary doughnuts on it. Still, she was up for the challenge. "But, if Reginald had done this," she said, "surely he would have been caught?"

"Well, then there was the fire, which pretty much finished the business, and Aretha's parents died," Mangus said. "So, even though they inherited, they didn't inherit anything of any great value."

"But the insurance would have paid out," she said.

"Not on the jewels, as they didn't have any proof of the stock value. Only a rider to say the amount they kept on hand on an average day. Not for this extra shipment. And, once the building burned, without any insurance coverage whatsoever, they didn't have anything left."

"Is that when Reginald died?"

"A few years after that. He had changed. I used to go down there every once in a while, get my watch fixed, get my wife the odd piece of jewelry. After the fire, there was just no other place in town with the same quality. I remember seeing him at a pub, drowning his sorrows. He was rambling on about how his wife wouldn't let him off the hook and that she blamed him for everything."

"Everything?"

He nodded. "The theft, the fire, the bankruptcy. Everything."

"Wow," Doreen said. And then she thought about Aretha, the cold woman who had suffered so much. "She might very well have blamed him, and, if she ever found any proof, then, of course, that would make it that much harder."

"Always," he said.

"Did the parents commit suicide? Maybe despondent over the loss of their income, their business?"

"Don't think so," he said. "As far as I understood, it was a car accident."

"Interesting," she said. "But the Abelmans did inherit at that point, right?"

"Sure, but, like I said, they didn't inherit much."

"Right," Doreen said. "After all that trouble, everything would have been a big complicated mess."

"Unless, of course," Nan said, "and I'm just wondering here, but maybe the Johnsons were going after their son-in-law for destroying their business. Then maybe he burned it down in retaliation?"

"And that would only happen if they had any reason to suspect him," Doreen said. She kept trying to twist all the parts into their rightful places, but, so far, she didn't have enough. "What I wouldn't give to see some of the insurance forms from back then."

"I've still got a lot of the boxes from my brother's company," Mangus said. "You're welcome to look through them."

Doreen stared at him. "Why would you have the boxes?"

"Because my brother saved everything from the business because he wanted his sons to step in. But neither of them had the interest or the aptitude, and at least my brother was smart enough to understand that."

"So why did you end up with the boxes when it was sold? Why didn't it all go with the business?"

"This is a lot of historical stuff. He'd already had it all scanned, so digital copies exist in the cloud storage somewhere," he said, emphasizing the internet way of doing business, as if it were something completely foreign. "I told him not to get rid of the paper files, just in case, and that I could store them, so he had a backup."

"But he's been gone quite a few years now, hasn't he?"

"Yep," he said. "The thing is, I've put everything into

storage. I have one of those big storage units, and one of these days when I'm gone, my poor family will have to empty it out." He shook his finger at her. "But, if you want, you can get those boxes and see if you can figure anything out."

"I'd love to see if I could," Doreen said. "Any idea how many boxes we're talking about?"

He gave her a fat smile. "A dozen or so."

She groaned. "Oh, no."

"Oh, yes," he said, laughing. "Besides, it's not like you have anything else to do."

"Well, I was trying to finish my gardening so I could get a deck built, but I'm still struggling to get the supplies."

"Oh, good," he said. "Tell me more."

And, just like that, the entire conversation switched to her deck addition.

"I think I've got it down to about four hundred dollars now," Doreen said. "But it doesn't seem like enough material for that much of a drop in my estimate. So I'm not too sure yet. It will probably be at least twice that."

"I wouldn't be at all surprised," Mangus said. "Once you start a project like that, the costs just keep rising. Budgets get thrown out the window, and you're lucky if you even finish the dratted thing."

Chapter 17

Monday Noon ...

B Y THE TIME the brunch was over, Doreen still didn't
have concrete information, but now she had a dozen
boxes to collect. Mangus had offered to have them pulled
from the storage unit and sent to her home, and she'd been
grateful to hear that. She asked him what she should do
when she'd finished with them.

"Shred them all and put them in the recycling bin."

She nodded in agreement. She didn't know when she
would be getting the boxes, but it wouldn't be a good day for
her when she had to go through a dozen or more of them,
filled with potentially useless paperwork. On the other hand,
she wasn't sure how to figure out what was going on
otherwise. She did like the theory that Reginald had been to
blame for all the problems, but, at the same time, that was
also a simplistic answer. And the store had gotten a lot of the
jewels back, but had they gotten all of them? She didn't
know. It seemed to her somebody who was part of that
whole shebang had tried to save a bag of jewels and had put
them away for later. Maybe either Reginald or Aretha.

Would Aretha have been a part of it? Doreen hoped not,

but it was possible Aretha's husband had been—both of them actually. Now if only Aretha would talk to Doreen about it. What were the chances these jewels were Aretha's? And, if that were the case, Aretha needed them, and she needed them badly. But she wouldn't get them unless they were really hers. Doreen would have to wait and see just what came from Mangus's boxes.

All kinds of information could be there, but Doreen didn't know what business documents had to be handed over for an insurance policy to cover that level of coverage. Was it just stock to be replaced or was it loss of business? And then you had to prove it.

She wandered home slowly, and she couldn't stop thinking about it. She had barely hit the property line when her phone rang. It was Zachary Winters again. "Hello," she said.

"Hi. Did you think about my offer?" Zachary asked.

"No," she said. "I already told you the answer is no."

"Sure," he said. "But you know what? I drove past your house, and it's obvious you can use the funds."

"I'd like to know how you found out about the jewels," she said.

"Oh, you know, great finds are great for spreading information," he said.

"Maybe," she said, "but they're not very good for building confidence."

"Confidence is overrated. As long as I pay the money, what do you care? You could be tens of thousands of dollars richer."

"But I'd like to know who they belong to."

He stopped and said, "Wait. They're not yours?"

And she realized her gaffe. "Yes, they're mine, but they came from somewhere."

"So you don't know the history of them?" he asked, his voice suspicious.

"You mean, you're asking for its provenance now?" she asked in a caustic tone. She'd had more than enough of dealing with provenance after all Nan's antiques had been uncovered.

"Oh, okay," he said. "I understand now that you ended up with them."

"Yes, you could put it that way," she said.

"Even better reason for me buying them off of you."

"And how do you know they are of such good quality?"

"Because somebody told me they are."

"That just comes back to the jewelry store where I took them to be appraised. Who leaked it? Mindy or Jeremy? I could have their businesses collapse over this. Sharing confidential information is unethical."

"I don't think so," he said. "Besides, if you accept the money, then we're all happy."

"Maybe not," she said. "There's a price for silence."

"What? So now you want a higher price for them?" And it was his turn to get disgusted.

"And yet you seem to think you're offering me a fair price," she said.

Then his next offer had her eyebrows shooting up.

"Are you telling me that isn't enough?" he said. "If you invest that, you'll be just fine for a while."

"Maybe," she said, but all she could think about was Aretha. Doreen hated the fact she could sympathize with and relate to the woman.

"We figured these were involved in a robbery from years ago anyway," Zachary said.

"And how do you figure that?"

"Because a lot of high-end jewels went missing many years ago, and they were never recovered. We think these might be part of that haul. As there was no insurance on them, there weren't any appraisals to go by all these years."

"I guess that makes sense," she said.

"Insurance companies tend to contact other jewelers, gem setters, and jewelry makers to let them know when things are stolen. Because, once they're stolen, then they can become a whole different item. And, of course, they should be returned to the police."

"Interesting," Doreen said. "I don't suppose you have any of those old alerts, do you?"

"Maybe," he said, his tone curious. "But they're yours legally, aren't they?"

She smiled. "Yes."

"Do you have proof?"

"I'd like to see your alerts first," she said.

"Give me your email, and I'll send them to you. I really am interested in buying them."

"You can get jewels anywhere, so why do you care so much about these?"

"I'd like the emerald in particular. I figured I'd have to buy the whole lot to get it."

"Why that one?"

"Because according to the person who told me about it, it looks to be a match to one I have that I bought for my wife a long time ago. We ordered the second one, but it never came in."

"Who did you order it from?" she asked calmly, but she waited with bated breath.

"Johnson and Abelman," he said.

"That must have been a long time ago."

"Yep," he said. "We've been married a lot of years, and I've always wanted to get it for her."

"You've been hanging on to the first emerald this whole time?"

"Yes," he said. "This was supposed to be a match for hers."

"Does she care now?"

"She cares," he said. "She cares a lot."

"Send me the alerts, and let me take a look."

"Sure," he said. "Remember. If it's one of those, then by rights the police have to be informed."

"Don't worry about the police," she said. "It's already been cleared."

"Interesting," he murmured. "Like I said, I still want it."

"I hear you," she said, "and I want those alerts."

"I just sent them to you. Call me." Then he hung up.

Chapter 18

AS SOON AS Doreen walked into her house, she sat down before her laptop. Overly full, and definitely not needing anything else to spike her energy, like coffee, she brought up her email. Sure enough, she had a new message. As she opened the file, she found a scanned copy of a page from a long time ago. Somebody must have kept them. This was an alert about the Johnson and Abelman Jewelers robbery and quite a few jewels that had gone missing. There was a brief description of the types of jewels and an ugly blurred image on the top of the page. Of which could describe what she'd found—or rather some of it could match up.

There was no follow-up on it, but then it was possible Zachary wasn't sending everything to her. Maybe some of these alerts were sent from the jewelry company itself? Hoping to nudge someone into handing over the gems? As she looked at the page, she noted it came from Hobart's Insurance Company. So, if the boxes coming from Mangus had something similar in its files, there could be one saying some of the jewels had been found.

She printed this one off and, at the same time, forwarded the email to Mack. Her phone rang right away.

"This is interesting," Mack said.

"Why would the police have returned the jewels to your mother if they matched those in the theft? And, no, I don't know that they did, but the image I forwarded to you got me thinking."

"The most important reason would be they couldn't prove the jewels came from that theft," he said. "I'm still looking for the case file on that."

"Yeah," Doreen said, a note of suspicion in her voice. "This is getting a little hinky."

"Don't start making assumptions," Mack warned. "Remember. We do better than that."

"You do," she said, "but I'm still stuck wondering about the hows and the whys."

"Interesting that he contacted you."

"The appraiser, Jeremy, called Zachary," she said. "Jeremy's the one who picked up the big emerald and checked it over." As she was talking to Mack, more emails came in from Zachary. "Hang on," she said. "He's sending me more stuff. And, indeed, one is a scanned copy of a handwritten order for the emeralds. Then a follow-up note from the jewelry store, showing the delivery of the first one and the second one on order. I'm forwarding these to you," she said in excitement. "It backs up Zachary's story."

"And yet," Mack said, "why and how did they end up at my parents' place?"

"I'm pretty sure, based on what Mangus *assumes*," and she put careful emphasis on that word, "that Aretha's first husband was responsible."

"You think he arranged the theft himself?"

"For the insurance most likely," she said. "And then, with the fire, I don't know how much was reclaimed. I am getting some boxes from the insurance company though, from Mangus."

Mack sucked in his breath. "Unbelievable," he said.

"Maybe." Just then her doorbell rang, and Mugs took off barking. Doreen groaned. "Now I've got somebody at the door." She kept talking to Mack, as she opened the door to see a pickup out front. She looked at the young man while Mugs danced at her feet.

"Hi, I'm Mangus's grandson, Grantham," he said, "and apparently these boxes are for you." With that, he propped open the screen door and unloaded all the boxes into her living room.

"Thank God, there are only twelve boxes," Doreen announced to Mack, as the kid gave her a wave and took off.

Mack started to laugh. "Remember," he said. "If you find anything—"

She promptly hung up on him, glaring at the phone. "Not cool, Mack," she muttered.

Mugs was busy sniffing around the boxes, and even Goliath had hopped on top of one. Thaddeus, never to be outdone, hopped onto one of the boxes and pecked around, his head twisted, as if reading the lettering on the box.

Doreen pocketed her phone and looked at the boxes stacked up in no particular order, noting each one was dated. Dates going back forty years. She whistled. "Maybe it'll be easier than I thought," she said, and she pulled out the oldest of the boxes and noted it was taped.

Stepping into the kitchen, she grabbed a sharp knife, then went back and sliced open the top. Inside were not files, as she'd expected, but loose papers stacked on top of each other, including note cards and smaller cards that looked like they came from a little Rolodex. The boxes were big, much bigger than she was used to.

She emptied one box, keeping the papers in sequence and hoping some order was within the chaos. She was delighted when she saw most of the paperwork was in chronological order. The dates on the box covered a five-year period.

She was pretty sure such a company generated a lot more paperwork than this, so maybe these were just problem cases or cases that didn't get resolved. Not new clients or accounts with no claims or anything like that. As she worked through them, she realized that was exactly what this was. A collection of the troublesome cases. And the stack she had was mostly from Johnson and Abelman.

She sat down, leaning up against the box, and slowly went through the documents. The initial coverage, then the theft, for which there was a police report. She crowed with laughter at that. She pulled it out and got up, keeping the paperwork carefully in the same position and scanned it, sending it to Mack.

Then she replaced it, but this time with a sticky note sticking off the top. Then she went through the rest.

What followed was basically the logistics behind what she'd already heard. The break-in at the business, and a theft that hadn't been fully insured. A handwritten note contained comments, suggesting some dissension and in-fighting between the owners and more stock had been ordered than was necessary. One comment even indicated suspicions that the burglary was part of the problem and potentially was a setup.

Doreen found some missives back and forth, letters from

the Johnson family, trying to get coverage for all the stock that had been purchased and had gone missing, but, because they didn't have proof for a lot of it, even though they'd done their best to get copies of receipts, the insurance company wasn't prepared to cover the exorbitant amount. They had covered what had been in stock and, per their normal rider, a percentage of the business itself. But there was still contention, and they would have to go through dispute resolution over it. In fact, the Johnsons had even filed a lawsuit against the insurance company.

She found notes on the insurance company copy that indicated their lawyers had been contacted. As she continued through the documents, not more than two months later the fire occurred, ripping through the business. On that claim, the insurance company had balked about paying out any more because of the problems with the previous claim.

Doreen picked up that note, then scanned it and sent it to Mack. Then she added a sticky note to flag this page as important, put it back in order, and carried on. It was fascinating reading. In the end, the insurance company didn't have to pay out for the fire, and they hadn't paid out the full amount for all the jewelry either.

She wasn't sure that they had any kind of notation as to what went on in terms of the jewelry business itself going under, but it went bankrupt about the same time, and not all the creditors could be paid. Some of the jewels were recovered, and most of those were sold, including all the inventory that was salvageable, in order to help cover the debts, but the final result was, they were broke. As she got to the end of the box, she found it went on to other cases.

A single note said the lawsuit was dropped. The Johnsons, majority owners of the company, had died, leaving just

Reginald and Aretha holding the bag. Neither had the funds to carry on with a lawsuit, and another note said the case was closed. Doreen put an elastic band around all the paperwork that pertained to the Johnson and Abelman case, thankful she didn't have to go through the rest of the boxes. She did go through the rest of this box, just in case, but nothing else was connected to the Johnson and Abelman Jewelers company.

Picking up what she had found on the jewelry company, she took out each of the pages with the sticky notes attached, making duplicate copies of these sheets, reinserting them into the chronological stack, then double-checked for staples or paper clips in the rest of the paperwork, and ran the entire file through her scanner. When she was done, she reclipped it all together and put it back in the box. Then she closed it up.

With that safely in digital form and her notes in hand, she thought it all over, deciding she needed to talk to Aretha. And that wouldn't be fun. She groaned, knowing she might as well get it over with. "Okay, Mugs. How about a walk?"

Mugs barked and raced over to the kitchen, where Doreen apparently had left his leash. He dragged it back excitedly, flicking it around, until the end of the leash smacked Goliath, who then chased after Mugs, trying to attack him. Mugs yelped and dashed behind Doreen, trying to keep her between him and Goliath, who was still rightfully pissed.

Joining the crowd, Thaddeus landed in the center and cried out, "Thaddeus is gorgeous."

Doreen stared at her ridiculous menagerie and laughed. "Come on. A walk is just what we need. Hopefully it will change the attitude around here."

She gathered them around her, and, after securing the front and back doors, walked to Heidi's. Doreen saw no sign of Heidi in the gardens, and the gates were locked. Doreen found a button to push though, and, shortly after she did, Aretha's voice answered from inside.

"Aretha, it's Doreen."

"What do you want?" the woman asked, sounding exasperated.

"I'd like to talk to you about the jewelry business and the insurance problems at Johnson and Abelman."

There was shocked silence on the other end. "Why would you want to do that?" she asked.

"Because I think it's important," Doreen said, speaking gently. "I think I know a lot about what happened, but I'd like to hear the truth from you."

"Does anybody even know what the truth is?" Aretha asked, her voice sounding tired and old. But she hit the buzzer and released the lock on the gate, so Doreen could come in. As Doreen headed up to the house, she studied the gardens and smiled because they did look so much better. At the front door Aretha stood waiting.

"Why are you putting your nose into my business?" Aretha snapped. For all her regal stance, her clothes were from a decade ago, and her features showed strain and stress.

"Are you feeling okay?" Doreen asked gently.

Aretha gave an irritated shrug. "Of course I am. What do you care anyway?"

"You might be surprised," Doreen said. She smiled at the older woman. "What can you tell me about what happened with the burglary?"

"Nothing to say," she said, her tone clipped. "We came in one day to find the windows were smashed and a lot of the jewelry was gone."

"Did you recover any of it?"

"Some of it was recovered, yes. Dropped and scattered all over. And that was all sold to pay the bills."

"But not all of it was recovered?"

"No. Not all of it." She hesitated but then firmed her lips, pressed them tightly together, and wouldn't say any more.

"Did you ever figure out who did it?"

Again came a haughty stare, and her nose cranked up another inch higher.

Doreen recognized the signs. She'd seen them in many of her associates in her previous life.

"No," Aretha said. "There were a lot of theories, and my parents certainly had a lot of their own at the time, but they were just trying to cause trouble."

"Did they blame your husband?"

Stunned, a surprised expression covered Aretha's face. Like a deer frozen in the headlights, she whispered, "How did you know?"

"Because he is the logical choice," Doreen said.

Aretha shook her head. "How is that logical?" she asked. "My parents helped him into the business. They showed him everything. It was just me in the family, so my husband knew we would inherit everything."

"But maybe he didn't want to wait until you inherited?" Doreen said. "Did you want more than he could afford? Was he feeling pressure to give you more?"

Aretha shook her head, bewilderment in her gaze. "No," she said. "We were fine."

"Did he want things? Did he want a fancy sports car or a bigger house? Could he have felt like the standard of living wasn't meeting his expectations?"

"He was a bit of a gambler," Aretha said, "and he always thought big. He wanted to have a cabin on the lake and a bigger house in town." She shrugged. "I just ignored him, figuring he was a bit of a dreamer."

"And what would it take for a dreamer to cross the line to theft," Doreen wondered.

"We were having some marital problems. But divorce was still a stigma I didn't want back then."

"Your parents would have been okay with it though, right?"

This time Aretha's gaze was haunted, but she nodded. "It's only as you look back over the years that you realize the mistakes you made," she whispered. "My parents, they didn't like him. They opened their arms to embrace him because they figured, if they didn't, they would lose me. And, after everything they did for my husband, it still seemed like it wasn't enough."

"And then you mentioned divorce, correct?"

"We had a big fight. I wanted to move out, to go back home to my parents. I told him I wanted a divorce."

"And the break-in? Was it that night or another night?"

"That night," she said. "I did go back to my parents' house. I left at ten o'clock, although I told the police I was home. I provided an alibi for my husband, but I really don't know if he was home or not."

Bingo.

"It's too bad you did that," Doreen said, "because some of this could have been resolved so much earlier."

"I don't know about that," she said, "but I felt I owed my husband that much."

"And yet didn't you wonder if he may have had something to do with it?"

The older woman hesitated.

Doreen nodded, encouraging her. "Of course you wondered. But, once the insurance didn't pay out, you guys were in financial trouble, weren't you?"

Aretha nodded. "My parents were devastated. Everything they'd worked so hard for, and now they wouldn't even have enough money for their own retirement."

"And then the fire?"

"Why are you dredging up all this?" Aretha said, visibly shaken. "Don't you see it's painful?"

"I'm trying to get it all straightened out," Doreen said. "It is important. Please trust me that far."

Aretha shrugged. "Maybe," she said. "The fire was the end of it. The insurance company wouldn't pay and were already calling us insurance frauds. It was a mess. They'd canceled the insurance on the business, but my parents didn't tell me."

Aretha sagged against the waist-high railing on the front porch. "That was too much for my parents."

"And they died soon after?"

"Yes, I believe so." The older woman reached up and pressed her fingers to her temples, as if the memories were painful.

"I'm so sorry for having to do this," Doreen said, "but did you ever wonder who set the business on fire?"

Aretha slowly raised her gaze and nodded. "I didn't have to wonder. I've always been sure it was my husband. He said something at the time I didn't understand. About not knowing it wasn't insured. But he never would tell me what he'd done. So I had no proof. Just that uneasiness …"

"Did you tell the police?"

She shook her head. "No, I didn't."

"Maybe you should have," Doreen said.

"We're going back to that decision I made such a long time ago," Aretha said, as she sagged even lower on the railing and stared out at the gardens. "Back then, I thought I was everything," she whispered. "I was raised in the highest of society, and, even though we worked in a trade, it was a wealthy trade. I knew everybody who was anyone and was privy to their secrets. I was privy to their world. My husband and I were both welcomed in society, but, after the fraud accusations, the fire, and then the death of my parents, it was all just too much."

"And, in all this, what happened to your husband?"

"I had to go back to our home after the break-in, or the police would have never believed the alibi. We stayed together for a time, but our marriage was going downhill. I did think afterward that he only hung around long enough to see if I would inherit anything."

"And?"

"My parents didn't have anything left to speak of," she whispered. "They'd already used up all their savings, their own money, and had even sold the house, though I didn't know it." Tears were in her eyes. "They did everything they could to pay back the people who had trusted them."

Doreen's heart ached for the older couple who would have realized how much they had lost. "I'm glad for them that they at least went to the grave thinking they had done the best they could," Doreen murmured. "But how terrible to know that their own losses and tragedies would continue to impact other people."

"Exactly," Aretha said, "it was a tough time, and Reginald was there for me."

"Good," Doreen said. But she wondered at the relationship. Had Reginald really been there for her or more for himself?

"But it also left me with nothing," Aretha said with a small smile.

"And your husband?"

"And then he died," she said with a bitter laugh. "At the time I couldn't decide if I was delighted or horrified, but I knew I wasn't grief-stricken. Not about Reginald. I was still dealing with the grief over my parents."

"But some time passed between his death and theirs, didn't it?"

She nodded. "Yes. A couple years between them. But I was very close to my parents. That loss remained with me a long, long time. At the time, I was trying to find a way to get away from my husband. He'd taken everything I had and had crushed it all to powder."

"Did you ever suspect maybe he had stolen some of the gems for later?"

"I asked him if he had because I couldn't let the idea go," she said. "He just looked so hurt that I ended up feeling guilty." She shook her head. "I found out later he had stolen quite a few of the gems and had hidden many of them in places I would never find." She shrugged. "He left me a strange letter before he died, saying gems were still hidden in the city, but he couldn't find them anymore. The landmarks he'd written down to remind himself were no longer there, so he didn't even have a way to get them himself."

"Why would he have left you that letter?"

"Because he'd kept some of the jewels and slowly sold them over time, after we were separated," she said bitterly. "He had essentially lived off my family for all those years, and, when he finally ran out and knew he would be done for, all he wanted was that last bag of jewels, but he couldn't find it."

"Do you know how many gems were in the last bag?"

She shook her head. "No, I don't remember. Only that this last group had an emerald he didn't dare sell because it had been specially ordered by a friend of mine for his wife." She shook her head. "It was so hard to hold my head up in society."

"Was it helpful when your husband died?"

"I don't know about helpful, but it allowed me to close a chapter. A long and sordid chapter I was desperate to be done with."

"And even if some jewels do show up," Doreen said, "there's no way to prove whose they are, is there?"

"No, probably not. The whole thing was a mess with many clerical errors, which is why the insurance wouldn't pay on that group of stones, as they couldn't be proven to have been part of the shipment or that they were in our possession. The only way would be if the emerald happened to be with them."

"Why is that?"

"It was a very specific emerald that was custom ordered. Records exist for that. But not that it was ever received."

"Do you know who ordered the emerald?"

The older woman smiled and nodded. "Yes, I do," she said. "It was an old friend, like I said. His name is Zachary. Zachary Winters."

Bingo.

Chapter 19

Monday Afternoon ...

DOREEN LEFT SOON afterward. She hadn't told Aretha about the jewels Millicent had found. Still, too many unanswered questions were here. Not the least of which was the question of whether any crimes had been committed that mattered today. If those jewels were from the store, did they belong to Aretha? Did they belong to the insurance company? Or did they belong to Millicent because she had turned them in to the police and then had them returned again? Doreen just didn't understand enough about how that worked. She would have to talk to Mack. But she realized for the first time that she and her animals had found no dead bodies related to this case. Wouldn't that be nice for a change? She skipped along the road with the animals, quite cheerful at the thought of making so much progress.

As she walked toward her driveway, she saw a strange vehicle, which looked like a Lexus, parked in front of Richard's place. She frowned at that, but, as she got closer, a man stepped out, and she recognized Jeremy, the appraiser from the jewelry store. With her hands on her hips, she glared at him. "Aren't you a lousy piece of work?"

He flushed. "This friend of mine has been looking for that emerald for a long time," he said.

"Interesting," she said, "and I get that. But you should not be leaking information. Confidentiality is everything in the jewelry business."

"It is," he said, "and Zachary told me that he's contacted you several times."

Doreen nodded. "That's correct. And?"

He hesitated and said, "If you ever want to sell it ..."

"You didn't even tell me what it's worth," she said. "Not that I can trust anything you say now. And, by the time I'm done letting everybody know what you did—"

"Wait," he said, holding up his hand. "It was only in this extenuating circumstance."

"Why is that?" Doreen sneered. "It was forty years ago."

"Zachary and I knew each other back then. He was my best friend's father."

"How do I know you didn't steal them to begin with?"

"Look. I didn't know him when all this happened, but he told me that he'd been hunting for the emerald a long time. He contacted the company it was ordered from and learned it had been shipped to Kelowna. So he knew it was here in town and just hoped it would show up one day."

"So, why is it so important, even after all these years?" she asked. "It's just an emerald."

He smiled. "Just an emerald to you maybe. But you have to understand his wife was everything to him."

"Past tense?"

"Will be soon," he said. "She's got cancer, and he's afraid she won't live too much longer."

"So what difference does the emerald make then?" she asked curiously.

"It's been eating away at the two of them all this time. If nothing else, they want closure."

"And, if he can," she said with a nod, "he wants to buy it and finally give it to her. Is that it?"

"Well, the treatments are ongoing, and he's hoping she'll pull through, and they'll have another twenty years. Either way, he would like to finish something he had promised her way back when."

"Does she have the other one?"

He nodded. "He had it set in an earring, and it's waiting for this one."

"And you think that's the one I had you take a look at?"

"I'm positive," he said. "I've identified and appraised the other one several times. I know they're a matched set."

"Interesting," she said. "I'll think about it."

He hesitated.

She glared at him. "Don't pressure me."

"They'll pay a good price."

"I heard you," she said, "and I said I'll think about it."

"Already more lives have been damaged than we ever realized from this."

"Meaning?"

"Meaning, when the store had the break-in, then the fire, and then going belly-up, it impacted not just the Johnsons directly but everybody else too."

"Meaning, the people who had ordered the jewelry had hopes and dreams of their own."

"And a lot of the creditors took a hit."

"It sounds like the Johnson family took the biggest hit," Doreen said. "They lost everything."

"I know. And for that I'm sorry."

"I think everybody's forgotten about Aretha."

He nodded. "That's possible. She did remarry, so everybody assumed she was okay. The problem is, the theft is so old that not many people care anymore."

"I don't think anybody can assume that," Doreen said quietly. Inside her head, Doreen was screaming, *I care. I care.* "Like I said, don't push me." And she turned and walked up to her house, letting herself and the animals inside. Then she walked to the living room window to watch him drive away. She released her pent-up breath. "We really need to talk to Mack about this one."

That we do, she answered herself. She headed into the kitchen and poured herself a cup of ice tea. Sitting outside on the deck with her notes, she tried to focus. Some of it was pretty self-explanatory, and it appeared all the culprits were dead. And maybe that was all that mattered. Maybe all that remained was that people needed to deal with their losses.

Then she thought about the Johnsons, wondering if they had committed suicide with their car accident. And then she thought about Aretha's husband. Had he died on his own?

She had been sitting here only twenty minutes or so when the doorbell rang. Mugs, already tired and frustrated, was busy barking at the front door, letting the world know there was an intruder.

Doreen opened the front door, surprised to see an older man. "Zachary Winters, by any chance?"

He beamed. "That's me."

"Well, I'm not inviting you in," she said.

His face fell. "I can understand that. It's not that I'm trying to rush you—"

"But you're trying to rush me," she said. "I need to talk to the police about this."

"Oh." He stopped and stared at her.

She shrugged. "I like to do things properly, so go away and leave me alone for now. As long as nothing criminal is involved, then I'll be happy to consider your request."

"I don't know much about it, but I doubt anything criminal was done," he said. "I know the Johnsons died in a car accident a long time ago. Even if somebody did try to kill them, that person is probably not around anymore."

"If somebody did, my vote would be for Reginald Abelman, their son-in-law."

He snorted at that. "Slimy little bugger, yes," he said. "I'd have voted for him too."

"I'm still figuring it out."

He shrugged. "If there's anything I can do to help, let me know."

Pulling out her phone, Doreen hit Record. "You can start by telling me exactly what happened."

Lifting his eyebrows, he said, "Not a whole lot to say. We ordered the twin emeralds, my wife and I. It was so great when we were called in. I was so excited. In the end, we approved one, but the second emerald had a flaw in it. It just wasn't good enough. That's why they wanted me to come in again. So they sent it back and ordered a replacement. We waited and waited, and finally we got a phone call, saying it was in. The next morning we arrived to find the police there and the business shut down, due to a break-in the previous night. At that moment, I knew it was gone."

"Did you talk to anybody about the emerald?"

"Just my wife and I," he said. "Well, and Abelman, of course. He's the one we'd talked to before."

"Interesting," she said. "And then what happened?"

"We left. We had hoped the jewel thief would be caught, and the jewels recovered, and then, the next thing I know, a week, maybe two weeks later, the business burned up. That was followed by bankruptcy, the tragic car accident, and then sometime later, Abelman died as well."

"Any idea how Reginald died?"

"I believe he committed suicide," he said.

She nodded. "Like I said, I'm not ready to make a decision on that emerald yet, so you can head out."

He replied with a bark of laughter. "If it wasn't for that emerald separating you and me," he said, "I think I'd like you just fine."

Chapter 20

Monday Late Afternoon ...

DOREEN CLOSED THE door after speaking with Zachary Winters but stood to the side of the big window in her living room, so she could watch him leave. It wasn't that she didn't trust him; it was just that everything was blowing up in her face, and she wasn't sure who was involved and what everybody's agenda was. All she knew for sure was that she had one agenda, and that was to solve the mystery Millicent had given her. But Doreen still wondered who really did own those jewels. There was money involved, apparently a decent amount of it, but she wasn't sure how much. But for anyone who was broke, any money was a boon.

Millicent didn't appear to want anything to do with it, but that didn't mean Mack wasn't interested. And then there was Aretha.

Shaking her head, Doreen wandered into the kitchen and outside onto the deck. Enough of the afternoon sun was still out for her to sit and relax, as she pondered the big slash of dirt in her backyard where tarps had yet to be placed and where cinder blocks were to be laid down. She wondered if the blocks should go first.

She had a lot of things to consider with her deck expansion, and what she didn't want was to end up with long grass coming through her deck boards if they let just-enough light through for things to grow underneath.

And then she had to wonder about lights and shadows and deception.

Was Reginald Abelman really that foolish? If he was overeager, young, and ambitious, then, yes, potentially. If he'd engineered the theft, what had happened to all the other jewels? Who had he sold them to?

She almost wished the brothers who had been involved in Crystal's kidnapping were available to talk to. She bet they would know who could have fenced the jewels. Or at least might have known what direction to point her to. This all happened before their time, but she felt they'd have some idea, being in the B&E business. It was all such a mystery to her. And, of course, Crystal's father had run a pawnbroker business. He might have fenced them. But would he even have anything to say? Then again, he probably wasn't close to old enough. She was grasping at straws. Looking for someone to talk to. And coming up empty.

As she sat down with another glass of tea and pondered all of what she had learned, Mack called. She filled him in on her conversations with both the appraiser and with Zachary Winters.

"So it was the emerald from that burglary?" he said, his voice thoughtful. "And, of course, the case file wasn't very extensive."

"A lot of jewelry here is listed as part of the insurance claim, but Abelman didn't have it on their store inventory."

"And apparently it wasn't insured enough anyway. I did check into some of the notes we have here. The insurance they were supposed to have was an *extra* rider covering jewels that were in shipments, and they didn't have that."

"The Johnsons also weren't expecting the large order coming in," she said. "Apparently Abelman ordered it all without their knowledge."

"It's almost as if he was trying to make the business go under."

"And yet he was benefiting from the profits. So how does any of this make sense?"

"It doesn't yet," Mack said, "but I'm sure, with a little more digging, you'll figure it out."

"Maybe," she said. "I'm a little tired and, well, frustrated."

"Of course you are. It sounds like you had a pretty big day. How did your breakfast with Mangus go?"

"It was tea and treats," she said with a laugh. "And I had way too much sugar, among other things, but Mangus is a fascinating guy."

"Anything else come out of those boxes?"

"I haven't had a chance to look at the other eleven boxes. I scanned and emailed you a bunch of stuff earlier. But now? Well, now I'll spend the rest of the day just thinking about all this and hoping I can find a way to fit it into a puzzle that shows a picture. At the moment they're disjointed odd shapes."

"I'll leave you to it," he said.

"Wait," Doreen said. "What about your case? Anything new on the old women?"

"Still waiting on the autopsies."

"Anything else interesting happening?" she asked hopefully.

"For you, no," Mack said, his tone allowing no argument. "For me, lots, so I better get back to it." On that note he hung up.

She snorted down at her phone. "Of course *for you*," she said. "You just don't realize how lucky you are that I'm not in the same office. Imagine if we worked together." She gave a short laugh.

At that moment, Mugs plunked himself down on her feet. She reached down to scratch him. "Not too sure what's going on, buddy," she muttered. He gave a light *woof* and rolled onto his back, as if to say the only thing that mattered was that his belly got scratched. She gave him several moments of attention, then realized Goliath was wandering through the garden, stopping to sniff all the plants she'd gotten from Heidi. And that was a good reminder. They probably needed more water.

As soon as she stood, Mugs jumped onto his feet, and the two of them walked to the garden. Thaddeus somehow had ended up on the pile of rocks she'd cleaned out when she had been weeding. His perch was precarious at best, but he was watching Goliath steadily. She stepped up closer to the plants, checking how they were holding up. Then she got the hose and gave them more water.

In the heat, transplants always suffered. It was much better to transplant in the spring or the fall, on a cool cloudy day, but beggars couldn't be choosy. She'd take what she could get for free right now. As it was, she'd gotten a lot of beautiful plants for nothing but a little sweat equity. At least one side of the garden was now flush. She could wait a couple years and just move things over and match it all against Richard's side of the property, but it would be nice if she had some things over there now. And, of course, a few older things were there, and that side was planted more heavily than the side she had put all the new plants in. Maybe she had enough now.

She pondered that as she wandered up and down the garden, gently soaking it all. She still wanted the big patio blocks to get down to the garden, and maybe a little square down there at the end, where she could put a chair and watch the creek. There was room.

Closer to the creek, she eyed the height and noted it was back up to the highest point she'd seen it yet. It was fascinating to watch the ebb and flow of water. It wasn't an ocean with a moon affecting its tides. Instead, it was water melting up in the mountains and other tributaries flowing into her little creek to make it the river it was just a few blocks away, but still the ebb and flow of majestic motion just fascinated her. As long as it stayed well below the height of her basement or down below her garden level, she was okay with it doing its own thing. She shut off the water to her hand nozzle and walked to the creek to see if the pathway was still clear. And, of course, it was.

She smiled and looked from the creek, staring back at her gardens, her eye critical as she studied the health of the plants, the layout of the planting, as well as that of the other side. Though she did get that other side weeded, she hadn't done any transplanting yet. She'd figured she would divide and conquer those big perennial masses come fall. And that would give her a little more time to decide on a better layout. What she should do was map what she had planted in the ground now, while she knew what it was, because, if the transplants suffered, she would have to cut them off a few inches aboveground and wait until they came out next spring. So it was quite possible she would completely forget what she had put in the ground.

Chapter 21

Tuesday Early Morning ...

DOREEN WOKE UP the next morning with an odd question in her head. How had Aretha found out her husband had stolen and was selling the jewels? She whispered it to herself out loud in the quiet room. All the animals were still sleeping in an array around her. She checked her watch to find it was only six. But that one statement kept playing in her head, over and over again.

It was possible her husband had told her. But, if that were the case, why leave her that letter at the end of the day? Doreen frowned, not sure whether she should contact Aretha and ask for clarification or just assume it was her husband taunting her with the information. And, if she did know, why hadn't she done anything about it? Why hadn't she gone to the police? Or had he been paying her to keep quiet?

With her thoughts going around in circles, Doreen tossed and turned in bed, wishing she could go back to sleep, only to finally give up and hop into the shower. She stayed under the hot water longer than necessary, just because it felt good. Her muscles hadn't produced the aches and pains she had expected, probably because of what she'd experienced when she had been doing Penny's garden not all that long ago. Maybe she was getting used to it, and her body was fitter and toned.

Still, once she was dressed, she picked Thaddeus up off his roost, with him squawking gently in her ear as they walked downstairs. Goliath was once again occupying his own perch on one of the bottom risers to her stairs, staring at her, his tail flicking, as if to say, *Don't even bother asking me to move because I ain't going to.*

She grabbed the banister and hopped over his step, but that left Mugs a step above. Goliath howled and Mugs barked, as she turned to watch the two face-off. She groaned. "Come on, Mugs. Just jump over him, like I did."

Mugs looked at her, then looked at Goliath, and did a half-hearted jump with his back legs catching Goliath in the belly, as they both slipped down the stairs onto the floor. Howling, Goliath jumped up and raced away.

Doreen laughed at their antics but headed straight for the coffeepot. She needed it today more than anything. She couldn't quite understand what message that early morning question was trying to prod from her brain. But, as she leaned against the counter and waited for a cup of coffee, she reminded herself how she hadn't been to the library on this case. And she really should go see just what information was available on the store and the family. There should be archives of newspaper articles, if nothing else. They were terrible to search for though.

She'd have to go through paper by paper, but still Kelowna only had the one major paper. Of course now everything was digital, so there were a couple competing new sites, but back then, forty years ago, there was only the one. Any major news from here would also have been picked up and noted in the *Vancouver Sun* paper.

As soon as the coffee was done, she poured herself a cup, nudged open the rear kitchen door, and stepped out onto the deck.

Goliath raced out and headed toward the same plants he'd been interested in yesterday.

She frowned at that. "What is it about Heidi's plants that bugs you?" she asked. "Is it just that they are different?"

Mugs barked at her several times, as he wandered through and lifted his leg on one in particular. She scolded him for it because a urine burn like that could kill a young transplant.

She raced over and watered it, trying to rinse it off and to thin down the urine. Mugs walked back to the grass with an offended air.

Goliath, on the other hand, wove through each of the transplants, marking each of them with his fur. She didn't understand that at all.

Knowing she couldn't go to the library without real food first, she headed inside and made some toast. As soon as the animals came in for their food, she would lock the doors and head out. She'd wasted enough time already that the library should be open when she finished eating.

Sure enough, by the time she was done and had the kitchen cleaned up and her second coffee down, she fed the animals so she could slip out easily. She grabbed her purse and headed toward the garage, locking all three animals in the house and resetting the security system. She backed down the driveway and headed to the large library only a few minutes away. As she pulled in to park, the parking lot was empty. However, the parking lot for the huge fitness center in the same area was overwhelmingly stuffed.

She groaned, muttering to the air around her, "Like I need that with my gardening projects." Turning her back on the big fitness center looming before her, she headed into the library and smiled at the librarian.

This librarian, younger than the one Doreen often saw in the evening, looked up with a smile. "Aren't you out bright and early this morning?"

Doreen just nodded and smiled, then headed to the back corner, where the microfiche was kept. She settled down to work, determining the years she needed to search through. It was not the easiest task, but she had a cup of coffee with her, even though it technically wasn't allowed. It was a travel mug that closed completely, so she had kept it in her bag the whole way, but she took it out now and placed it on the table beside her, slowly working through the newspapers with her notepad at the ready.

She found several articles about Aretha's marriage, about the burglary, followed by the fire, and the bankruptcy. They all had the same information though. She took screenshots of each, so she had the information for later, sending them off to her email. With that done, she went back and searched through the papers about Aretha's life, her parents, and then tried to find something on Abelman. She didn't have much about him yet.

Apparently he was relatively new to Kelowna, and his parents were from the lower mainland. In one of the articles though, she caught note of a sister. But the article was written so ambiguously, she wasn't sure if it was his sister or somebody else's. It came up several times, but still Doreen couldn't make heads or tails of it. Sometimes people wrote without defining who the subjects were clearly enough. She took a picture of it, so she could mull it over later. Nowhere else had she ever heard mention of a sister.

And, sure enough, none of the other articles said anything. She found nothing about the divorce, but there was a note about the car accident. It was just a simple black-and-white statement about the loss of an iconic local family. Both parents had perished in the crash. As Doreen kept reading on several years later, she very nearly missed it, but she found a byline in the obituary about Reginald Abelman. It didn't say suicide specifically though.

She frowned at that, took another photo, and kept going. She would have to confirm with Mack if it was a suicide. And she didn't know that Mack even had that information available. But who knew? In her heart she felt terribly sorry for Aretha's circumstances, but she also understood Nan's position about how Aretha, being a mean and difficult person, likely deserved everything she got.

Because of her own life, Doreen could understand how hard a shift it would have been, going from being a wealthy and prominent and well-respected woman, to suddenly being a nobody, now surrounded by scandal and drama.

Speaking of which, Doreen scrolled through, looking for mention of the insurance company. She found a few mentions of Hobart's Insurance Company but nothing major. Nothing about a court case either.

She wasn't at all surprised since that was hardly newsworthy, and, if the insurance company hadn't wanted anybody to pick it up, it probably would have been pretty easy to squelch a story. They obviously wouldn't pay a claim, or a lawsuit, if they didn't have to, and those million little footnotes on insurance policies would get them out of having to pay for all kinds of things. She did find a marriage notice for Aretha again, just a simple little notification. She took a photo of it though because it gave Doreen dates and times, and she marked it all down on her notepad.

She scrolled aimlessly for another forty-odd minutes, then realized she just wasn't picking up anything new. And once she ran out of microfiche, it would go to digital anyway. She took another big sip of her coffee, packed her notepad away into her big purse, then lifted the cap off her coffee and drank the last of it, since it was cool now.

Stowing the cup in her purse, she got up and decided she probably ought to pick up a couple books. At least something to justify her time here.

As she wandered up and down the aisles, she thought she heard somebody whispering. She peered through the books to the other side to see two women with their heads together, both gray-haired ladies, talking. As Doreen got closer, it was like they sensed somebody was here, and they broke apart.

Doreen came around the corner with a bright smile. "Oh, look, I'm not alone after all," Doreen said happily. "This place seemed like a graveyard this morning."

Both women just looked at her.

She smiled, shrugged nonchalantly, and said, "Sorry. I didn't mean to disturb you," and she went past them, looking down more aisles of books.

They happened to be in the biography section. Something she had never really gotten into. She couldn't understand why she should read books about other people's lives. It would just make her feel worse about her own. It always seemed like other people were doing things, living life, whereas she was just existing. Too bad there wasn't a biography section for local Kelownians—now that would have been interesting.

On that note, she walked over to the librarian and asked

if there was such a section. The woman looked at her in surprise and then nodded. "We do have a small group of books on that topic." She led her to a different section that was all about Kelowna.

With a smile, Doreen thanked her and took a look. And, sure enough, there was one on the journalist Bridgeman Solomon's life. She snatched that book and smiled. "I thought bios were written *after* people died. It's hardly fair when you're still hanging on to the last threads of your life," she said, "but, hey, this might give me insight into why you ended up doing the kind of work you did."

With that book in hand, she picked up one of the new releases prominently displayed on a big shelf where she first walked in. It was a good author, and she would enjoy it. She took her two items to the front desk, where she was checked out. She leaned closer to the librarian. "I know I'm relatively new here, but I was just wondering who the two ladies were who were here."

The librarian smiled. "That was Mrs. Applegate and Mrs. Gundon. They come almost every morning."

"Ah," Doreen said. "It sounded like they were gossiping more than looking for books."

"I think they come here just to do that," she said. "Both of them have husbands who aren't very interested in reading, so this is their way of getting out for a bit."

"You should open a coffee shop inside the library," Doreen said. "You guys would make a killing."

"We're run by the city," she said, laughing, "so we're constrained by all sorts of government rules and regulations. A coffee shop is already in the mall, so we can't compete with them."

Doreen smiled, then laughed. As she headed outside, she

grabbed her notepad and jotted down the names, Applegate and Gundon. Interesting. Too little old gray-haired ladies, gossiping in the library. Doreen frowned as she thought about it, wondering about Mack's cases. She wished she knew more, but, of course, little old ladies tended to die when they hit the end of the road. There was nothing criminal about any of it.

She headed back to her car, dropped her books on the front seat, and drove home. As she pulled up into the driveway, another vehicle pulled up beside her. Frowning, she got out and walked to the truck parked on her driveway.

A stranger jumped out and gave her a smile. "You must be Doreen," he said, reaching out a hand.

She smiled. "I am, indeed. And who are you?"

"I work in dispatch," he said. "I got the word you're looking for decking materials."

Chapter 22

Tuesday Midmorning ...

DOREEN'S EYEBROWS SHOT up. "Absolutely," she said. "What have you got?"

"Mack said you're looking for decking boards and some more two-by-fours. I've also got a gallon of Varathane," he said. "That stuff is freaking expensive, but I don't have any more use for it. I did a deck for my mom in Vernon, and she insisted I take all the leftover materials away from her place. So now I've got all these extras and no use for them."

Doreen was delighted as she walked to the back of the truck to see quite a few two-by-fours and like six or eight decking boards. "You know what? At this rate," she marveled, "I almost have enough to do the job."

"Good," he said. "Because we all end up with leftover stuff, and it's a pain to hold on to or seems wrong to take to the dump. So we can't do anything but pass them on." He handed her a gallon that wasn't quite full but had quite a lot in it.

He said, "That's the stuff you need to treat the surface of these boards, if you want to. Particularly if you're putting up railings and stuff."

She smiled in delight, and then he handed her rollers and a paintbrush.

"Paint, you and I do not get along," he stated with a grin. "I don't want to keep these. I don't want them crowding up my garage. If you want to take that, I'll grab the wood."

And, good to his word, he stacked up the two-by-fours atop the decking boards. He must have done this for a living at some point because he took all of them out in one big swoop and put them on his shoulder. Doreen led the way to the side of the house and showed him the rest of what they had collected.

"This is looking mighty fine," he said. He put down his load and walked around to the backyard, where he could see the big area they had excavated the sod from. "That'll make a huge difference for you. You'll be able to put a table and chairs and even a barbecue grill on a deck that size." And then he saw the creek and smiled. "I had no idea these properties were on the river. That is beautiful."

"That's what I thought," Doreen said. "I just haven't had a chance to sit outside much and enjoy it."

"That's because you keep getting into everybody else's cases." He chuckled. "My name is Donnie, by the way, and I am an old friend of Mack's. I've heard about you two and all these cases you're closing."

"Well," she said, "I have to admit that I do love a good puzzle."

"You can always work on these dying old ladies," he said. "A third one dropped dead this morning."

Doreen stared at him in surprise. "Seriously?"

He nodded. "I took the call myself," he said. "Speaking of which, I promised Mack I'd get these supplies over here today. I wanted to do it right away so I didn't forget, but I'm going home again now to get some sleep. I work the grave-yard shift." He gave her a wave, hopped in his truck, and backed out of her driveway.

She was stunned, not only at his generosity in delivering these materials for her, but also the fact that a third little old lady had died. Immediately her mind went to the two in the library. She didn't know what was going on, but it was darn hard to ignore it all. She was fascinated, to boot.

She walked inside the house, letting the animals outside. Mugs had been barking like a crazy dog from inside because the stranger had been with her, and she hadn't let him out. She really hadn't had a chance to.

She went back to her car and unloaded the library books and grabbed her purse. She didn't want more coffee, but it would go so well with her newest research to do, now that she was further fascinated by these recent cases Mack was working. Her biggest concern was that, if somebody was targeting these older women, Nan might be in danger. Doreen did not want that at all.

She picked up her phone when she got back in the kitchen and texted Mack. **A third old lady died?**

He sent her a frowning emoji.

She smirked and texted back. **Yes, I heard.**

When her phone rang, and she answered, he snapped, "How?"

"How what?"

"How did you find out?"

"Donnie was here. He dropped off a bunch of two-by-fours, more decking boards, and three-quarters of a can of Varathane."

There was silence on the other end. "I gather he got the

call this morning," Mack said in a resigned tone.

"Yep," she said. "So this is of your own making."

"Not my making," he said. "I didn't have anything to do with the case."

"It's interesting though."

"No," he said. "It's not interesting."

"I suppose we have to wait to see if it's suspicious circumstances again?"

"Yes," he said. "Remember. Old people die all the time."

"Yes, but that's three gray-haired old ladies all in a row," she said.

"Not all that odd," he said. "It could be three gray-haired men next time."

"Maybe." She frowned. "Do you think something's going on?"

"I hope not," he said. "What have you found out?"

"The only new information I found on the gems, after spending hours in the library this morning, is that it looks like Abelman had a sister. It's mentioned once that his parents were in Vancouver with his sister. It's possible his sister came for a visit from time to time."

"That's possible," Mack said. "It doesn't really matter now though, does it? Since they're all dead."

"That's the problem with cold cases," Doreen said. "I can't get answers from a grave." And then she remembered something else she'd meant to ask him. "Speaking of which," she said, "is there any way to check Reginald's death certificate to see what the cause of death was?" She could hear him scratching down a note on the other end.

"If I can get to it," he said, "I'll take a look."

"Thanks. I just want—you know, like you said—to make sure I don't assume anything."

He gave a snort at that. "You assume way too much as it is."

"Maybe," she said, "but I'm learning." And, with that, she hung up on him this time.

She grinned, put down her phone, and headed out to her garden. The deck wouldn't get done by itself, and she needed to get as much other work done as she could, so she didn't waste time when Mack came to help her.

Several hours later she had almost all the garden weeded. She hadn't started the transplanting or dividing and splitting on the right-hand side yet, but she was looking at the rest of it, feeling like she was almost there. She'd taken the edger and gone around the section where the deck was and widened it a bit more. She wasn't too sure what to do with the step section but thought that would probably need something done with it too. She would wait on Mack for that. Then she got out the lawn mower, mowed everything, and marked off where she'd like to get some patio stones. While it was on her mind, she sent Mack a text. **Anybody got patio stones? I could use a path down to the creek.**

He just sent back a typical **LOL** answer.

She didn't know if that meant he would send out a message or not. She was likely to get a complete mix of blocks that way too, which may or may not work. She wasn't sure just how expensive concrete was. But she had been researching pouring individual blocks, thinking maybe that was an answer too. By the time she was done with everything in her garden for the day, with the lawn mower and her other tools cleaned up and put away, she felt tired again. She headed back inside, sat down with her notes, but the sister issue was really bugging her. She needed her name or something else to lead to the sister, but Doreen hadn't caught sight of anything yet.

Finally, out of desperation after spending an hour on research with no results, she sent Nan a text, asking if she would ask Mangus if he knew if Abelman had a sister.

And the response came back as **Will do**. But nothing else.

Groaning, Doreen got up, put on some coffee, and, although it was only four o'clock, she couldn't wait for food. She pulled out the last of the salmon pasta dish and warmed it up in the microwave.

When she sat outside on her little deck, she was closer to getting rid of it and having the new one built. She couldn't stop smiling. Until she realized they would also have a problem getting rid of the old deck materials too. She frowned at that, thinking that, after all this time, she might still end up making a dump trip.

She knew it was silly, but she also hoped it was possible to put electric lights out on the deck. Maybe she could have some lights for her laptop, so she could sit outside to work. She really didn't like the idea of running cords. She could keep her laptop fully charged and then use it outside, but she couldn't use her laptop in the sunlight and still see the screen. She wasn't sure what she was even looking for ultimately in her new deck, but so many beautiful decks were online, and the more she saw, the more she wanted. And that was a problem because, once you wanted a little bit, you could get greedy and want a lot more.

She had prided herself on avoiding a dump run so far, but this might just end up being the one time she would have to. And then she frowned and wondered if the old bed from the upstairs guest bedroom could go too. It would be great to send it off to some antique place, but she highly doubted anybody would want it. But then she remembered the heritage site she had handed off all the old nightclothes to.

She would have to remember to contact them and see if they were interested. In order to do that, she'd have to take pictures. It was a lovely bed, just not anything she wanted in her spare bedroom. She finished her dinner and looked sadly at her empty plate.

Well, I could warm up some more, she thought, but it would have to be straight noodles. Enough of those were left for another meal, and she didn't want to eat her dinner for tomorrow night a day early, leaving her with sandwiches again.

She cleaned her plate in the sink, snagged an apple, and walked upstairs to the spare room, her animals in tow. She took pictures of the bed from all angles, including one showing the maker's mark. Too bad Scott hadn't wanted it. She frowned. She had never shown it to Scott. She stood here, staring at it, and then thought she might as well send the photos to him.

With that, she went back downstairs, pulled up a new email, and sent a message to Scott. She put Antique Bed and Frame in the subject line and then attached the pictures from her phone. **Scott, I don't think I ever showed this to you. Not sure how it was forgotten. I assumed it had no value, so feel free to tell me that it doesn't, and I'll be happy to move it to the dump.**

She added a happy face emoji, signed it, and sent it off. With that done, she got up and did the dishes. She was restless though. And without a walk to Penny's and Steve's or Crystal's houses these days, Doreen felt a little at odds. But she wanted to go for a walk today, as she hadn't had a chance to get out and stretch her legs.

Chapter 23

Tuesday Late Afternoon ...

DOREEN CUT HERSELF a big wedge of cheese and snagged a second apple. She was being greedy perhaps, but she had burned up enough calories from her gardening work earlier today. Calling the animals to her, she headed out the front door and found herself walking right back down toward Heidi and Aretha's house. It was foolish of Doreen to go in that direction, but the gardens were beautiful, and, if she could get some more plants, then she would. But, of course, she was walking, so there wouldn't be much she could take with her.

As she sauntered down the street, she passed the big old house and smiled. It was such a beautiful, elegant home. She saw no sign of anybody outside working, but then it was evening. She walked past more houses, seeing beautiful gardens everywhere she went. It would be lovely to live in this corner of the world. There was just something timeless about it.

But nobody was out and about, no one to even say hello to. She turned around and headed toward home, the animals happy to go in any direction as long as they were out. When they passed Heidi's house again, Thaddeus started making an odd clucking sound. As she looked down, she saw Goliath, weaving in and out of all the plants in the garden bed.

"Goliath, get out of there," she urged. He just shot her a look and kept going. Mugs, his tail wagging like crazy, sat at her feet, as if to demonstrate how good he was being. She bent over and scratched him. Immediately Thaddeus cackled this weird *ah-ha-ha-ha* kind of a sound. She groaned. "I don't know what's the matter with you guys, but come on. Let's go home. You're a disgrace today."

"Doreen?" called out a happy, cheerful voice.

She turned to look, and there was Heidi. Doreen smiled and said, "Hi, Heidi."

"What are you up to?"

Preferring a white lie over sounding like an idiot, Doreen smiled and said, "Well, I headed out my front door to go for a walk, and I'm afraid these crazy animals led me here."

"Oh, isn't that lovely," Heidi said. She bent down to pet Mugs. Then she saw Goliath in the garden, and her smile fell away.

"I'm sorry," Doreen said. "I've been trying to get him out of there."

"Maybe you should consider a leash," Heidi said.

Doreen called Goliath, but he lay down in the mulch and just stared at her. She shook her head. "Normally he behaves himself," she said, "but tonight he's just being odd."

Heidi nodded and said, "He didn't go in the gardens last time, did he?" She looked around distracted. "Of course I might not have noticed, when I was so busy working."

"No, he was sunning himself on the concrete driveway," Doreen assured her. She felt uncomfortable because the animals were, indeed, misbehaving. Mugs now wandered closer and lifted a leg on the beautiful peonies. She tugged him back. "Don't you do that."

Heidi laughed. "Well, your hands are full. Have a good evening." She waved and headed back inside.

A little disappointed, Doreen waved back and called Goliath again. When he refused, she snagged him in her arms, which started Thaddeus arguing because the multiple positions were dislodging him from her shoulder.

When she finally straightened up, he spoke sotto voce, "Are you done?"

She stopped and twisted to look at him. "Did you just say that to me?" she gasped.

"*Ha-ha-ha-ha.*"

"Don't you do that," she warned.

"Are you done? *Ha-ha-ha-ha.*"

Astonished and aghast, Doreen stormed off. When she got to the end of the block, she stopped to turn back and saw Heidi in the driveway outside of the gate, watching Doreen. When their gazes met, Heidi turned around and raced away.

"Now look at what you did? Obviously the lady wasn't happy to have you in the garden," Doreen scolded Goliath.

Mugs barked.

"I get that," she said. "You were all being very difficult tonight. What was that about?" She got no reply and groaned.

When she reached her home, Mack was pulling up in her driveway. She watched him in surprise. "Wow," she said. "So many visits in such a short time frame."

He looked at her distractedly. "Mostly because everybody keeps bringing me shit," he growled.

She raised her eyes at his tone. "Like what?"

He pulled out two more cinder blocks. She laughed out loud. "We don't need those, do we?"

"We do if we're replacing your steps," he said. "And we'll need these all around the steps if we'll go without a railing too."

Doreen nodded. "I didn't think of that." She looked in the back of his truck to see more boards, all different shades. "Wow. Did they just bring you one board at a time?"

"These came from the captain." Mack shook his head. "Everybody seems to be interested in your deck."

"They're all welcome to come and help on the weekend," she said cheerfully. "The more hands, the better. I'll try my best, but I won't be as much help to you lifting a lot of this stuff, and you can't do it all yourself."

He just nodded but didn't say anything.

She smiled. "You look like you had a rough day."

"The damn cases," he growled. Turning to look at her, he asked, "Where did you come from?"

"Just from a walk," she said airily.

Mack dropped the cinder blocks on the side of her house, then went back and picked up the rest of the wood from the truck.

Thaddeus looked at him with a gimlet eye. "Are you done? *Ha-ha-ha-ha.*"

Mack stopped, turned to look at him, and said, "Seriously? Now I'll get attitude from the bird?"

"He's having an attitude moment," Doreen cried out. "I'm so sorry."

Mack rolled his eyes. "Where does he get this stuff from anyway?" He looked at her, the question written clearly on his face.

"Not me," she said. "I don't know where he gets it from.

He just said that tonight for the first time, when we were out on our walk."

"Where'd you walk to?"

"Down to Aretha and Heidi's place."

"Looking for more plants? I would think you had enough by now."

"I probably do have enough," she said. "But, when you're a gardener at heart, it's hard to turn down more."

"Did she offer you more?"

"No, she didn't. She was a little bit less friendly tonight."

"Well, it's nighttime," he said. "And, if you think about it, she was probably tired, like the rest of us."

She noted the fatigue pulling at him, the heavier wrinkles on his face. "I'm sorry," she said. "I keep forgetting you work a full-time job."

"More than full-time these days," he said.

She nodded, not knowing what to say.

He headed back toward his truck.

"Have you eaten?"

He nodded. "I had dinner, loaded up this stuff, and brought it over." With a honk of a horn, he took off.

She smiled and waved, then immediately felt lonely. Even worn out, he was such a vibrant life force, such a larger-than-life person, it was hard to ignore him.

As he drove away, she realized he hadn't answered her texts, any of the myriad questions that needed answering. Still another day had gone by with no answers, not even from Nan, and Doreen was getting frustrated. She was used to success, but this was starting to feel like a great big failure.

Chapter 24

Wednesday Morning ...

D OREEN WOKE UP Wednesday morning with a heavy heart. Something was just wrong with the information she had. She was missing something but didn't know what. As she got up and put on coffee, Nan texted her.

Mangus said he knew of a sister but doesn't know her name.

Good enough. Any idea who would?

No.

Another dead end. She hadn't had a chance to ask Aretha and wasn't sure she wanted to face Heidi and Aretha in their home either. Aretha was the one who would know, but how was Doreen to reach her? Just because Aretha had a sister-in-law didn't mean it had anything to do with this case. Doreen groaned though because none of this gave her any foresight into what she needed to do. She was getting frustrated and ugly about it. The days had just gone by, all blending into one another. And that was frustrating her more than anything. Deciding that getting an answer faster would be the best, she texted Mack and asked if he'd found out anything. About Jeremy. Zachary Winters. Reginald's cause of death. The three recent deaths of the old ladies.

No.

She winced at that. A *no* from Mack somehow came with a thunderous oppressive silence, versus Nan's chirpy birdlike no. They both meant the same thing; it was just so much easier to hear it from Nan. Doreen moved outside but found herself restless and out of sorts. She had checked the library and done everything she could. There didn't appear to be anything obvious online, although she had started searching for Reginald Abelman's name, looking for any sign there might be family. On a whim, she picked up the phone book and checked there. She found one.

Frowning, she picked up her phone and dialed the number. As an afterthought she checked her watch and hoped it wasn't too early to call. She didn't want to get people upset. But it was running on nine. When an older female answered, Doreen smiled to perk up her voice and dove right in with a direct approach. "Hello, my name is Doreen. I'm wondering if you are any relation to Reginald Abelman."

There was a pause on the other end. "Who's asking?"

She started again. "I'm Doreen," she said. "I live in Kelowna, and I was speaking with Aretha and was wondering if you were a Reginald Abelman's sister, who was her first husband."

"No," she said. "I'm not, but I find it so odd that you would ask."

"Why is that odd?" Doreen asked.

"Because, if I was his sister, you're assuming I wouldn't have married," she said, her voice snippy. "And I'm certainly not an old spinster."

Doreen's brows drew together; she had stepped on a land mine and didn't have a clue what had happened. "Oh," she said. "I meant no insult. I was trying to locate his sister, and there was always a chance she had been widowed or divorced and may have reverted to her maiden name. Or she could have remarried." She knew she was grasping at straws.

The woman on the other end gave a snort. "Then she could have any name," she said, her voice not quite as snappy but still enough so to make Doreen's teeth grind.

"Possibly, yes," Doreen said. "Really, I'm just trying to find any family members possible."

"Well," she said, "I'm not related."

With that, Doreen's shoulders sagged. "Oh," she said. "Do you happen to know of any other family members?"

Doreen could all but feel the laser gaze coming through the phone line.

"It's possible," the other woman said. "I'll have to think about it." Then she promptly hung up.

Doreen stared at her phone, wondering why that had gone so badly. Then she tried to figure out in what way this woman could know somebody who might be related. But then, if she had married a male with the Abelman last name, she wouldn't have been related, other than by marriage. At least she could be snippy and say, *Not related by blood.*

Doreen grabbed her notepad and wrote down the gist of the conversation, as well as the phone number. It was a fascinating thing to go into genealogy. She would love to do family trees, but it was so much easier to just do something on ancestry.com or another one of the DNA profile sites. She could see that being something people did automatically going forward. She'd have to check them all out herself. She didn't know how that worked. Also Reginald's parents had lived in Vancouver. She wondered if she could find records of them.

"I'm going crazy," she said to Mugs.

Mugs just sat back and woofed at her.

"That sounded a little too much like a yes," she said.

Just then the phone rang, and she looked at the number and groaned. "I'm not talking to you, Zachary." But the phone rang and rang. She waited until the voicemail kicked in, then listened to his message. It was the same as before. He really wanted the emerald for his wife. It was the perfect match and nothing less was good enough. She appreciated the fact that he wanted it, but how could she sell something she didn't feel was hers to sell?

The thought of getting ten thousand dollars for an emerald was great, but that wasn't the point. The point was, she'd been asked to figure out who the jewels belonged to and to return them to their rightful owner.

A part of her said they belonged to Aretha, but Doreen still wasn't sure about that. If Aretha had anything to do with any of the mishaps that had befallen her, then Doreen wouldn't give that money over to her, or the jewels for that matter.

Now Doreen was really out of sorts. Just as she got up to walk out to the garden and do something, her phone rang again. It was Zachary again. She hit Talk and then End Call, so she cut him off. She didn't want to deal with him right now. When it rang again, she went to do the same thing, but, recognizing another number, she answered it.

"I do know an Abelman," the snippy woman said.

"Good," Doreen said, letting out a long breath slowly. She walked back to the table. "Who is it?"

Silence.

"Is there a problem with telling me who it is?"

"Maybe," she said.

"Did she ever marry?"

"Yes."

Feeling like she was pulling teeth to get answers, Doreen took several calming breaths. "Is there anything you can tell me about her?"

"She lives in Kelowna."

"Okay, that's helpful," Doreen said, making a note. "Do you know what her last name is? Or did she have any children? Anything?"

"No, I can't say too much. No children though. And again, the last name would tell you who she is."

"Maybe," Doreen said, trying to hold back her exasperation. "I don't really understand why it's an issue though."

"Of course you don't," the woman said with a sneer. "That's because you're thinking about what you want. You're not thinking about what other people want."

Wincing at that because it was true, Doreen said, "You're correct. I am thinking about what I want. And I was hoping to get in touch with her."

"Is there any money involved?"

Her tone had changed, as if something were behind that question which Doreen needed to be careful of. Because, of course, the jewels were involved, but not necessarily to come to Reginald's sister or to this snippy caller. "I'm not sure why you would bring up something like that," Doreen said. "I'm not trying to pay her anything or charge her for anything either, for that matter," she added for clarity.

She heard almost a humming sound on the phone.

"Does she need money?" Doreen asked.

"Doesn't everybody?" the snippy woman said.

"Are you related to her?"

"No, but when she recognized my name, she mentioned

she had come from the same family line."

"The same family?"

"Only in that Abelman is a very old Jewish name," the woman said proudly.

"Ah," Doreen said in understanding. "And, of course, it's always nice to find other people who are connected in the family tree."

"Well, that's what I thought," she said. Then she added in a haughty tone, "Yet this woman isn't really connected. So she doesn't get the same treatment as family."

Chapter 25

Wednesday Midmorning ...

DOREEN NODDED, BUT, at the same time, she gave Mugs a big eye roll. "Well, if you could see your way to let me know what her last name is, or her first name, or where she lives, or her phone number, I would really appreciate it," she said. "I am not the police. I'm not a journalist. I'm not a creditor looking for money."

"Good thing," she said, "because she doesn't have any to give away. I'll have to think about it." And, once again, she hung up with a sharp *click*.

"Wow," Doreen said to Mugs. "The crazies are out in full force today." Of course that wasn't fair, but it suited the way she felt. "Why won't she just tell me who it is?"

But she hadn't. And that left Doreen wondering. She looked up the woman's address to see if that would tell her anything, but, of course, why would it? And then she looked up the Abelman name she'd gotten from the phone book and checked through the news. Again, another old distinguished family who had been here forever apparently, and, according to the bits and pieces she was reading, was one of the founding families involved in the communities for a good many years. They'd spawned four children, all daughters. All had married, and all had different names now. Which was why it was hard to find an Abelman name anywhere. But there was no relationship to Reginald or to his sister.

But this woman knew Reginald's sister. Doreen could just imagine a conversation where they'd meet up somewhere, and she'd introduced herself. What a shock to realize this person had the same family name you did. She couldn't imagine. Yet, at the same time, why wouldn't the woman tell Doreen anything?

Was this Abelman woman a criminal? Was she somebody in politics or one of those wealthy families always worrying about privacy? Not that Doreen had ever had to worry about privacy with her controlling husband. He'd always been very careful to keep everybody out of their lives, so it wasn't anything she had to worry about.

As she sat here, the phone rang yet again. She answered it to hear Mack on the other end.

"What are you doing?" he snarled.

Surprised, she stared at the phone. "What on earth are you talking about?" she asked. "I'm not doing anything."

"Oh," he said in surprise. There was a moment of silence.

"What did you think I was doing?" she asked curiously. "Because that was a pretty snarly attitude you tossed my way."

"I don't know. I just got a really bad feeling," he said.

Her eyebrows shot up. "Are you a psychic now?"

"It depends," he said, "if you're doing something stupid."

She snorted. "That's not funny."

"Neither is you getting into something you don't belong in."

"Maybe." Remembering the two old ladies she'd met in the library, she asked him, "Do you know Mrs. Applegate and Mrs. Gundon?"

He said, "Not that I know of. Why?"

"I don't know," she said. "It doesn't matter."

"What were you doing? I tried to call you a moment ago," he said. "The phone went to voicemail."

"I was talking to somebody in the Abelman family."

"You found Reginald's sister?" he asked in surprise.

"No, I found an Abelman in the phone book, so I called and got this really weird woman." She explained about the snippy woman and her conversation during the two calls.

"Well," he said, "lots of people like their privacy."

"I know," she said. "It just seems odd."

"You're looking for trouble where there isn't any."

She snorted at that. "You're a fine one to talk, considering what you said to me instead of *hello*. You're the one looking for trouble."

"In your case," he said with a hard sigh, "it's almost like there is no end to the trouble. But, if you're not doing anything, and you're sitting at home, staying out of trouble with the animals, then it's all good." And he hung up.

She snorted at that. "Jeez, Mack, you didn't have to start imitating me," she said to the empty room. But, of course, she was the one who had hung up on him so often that now he felt he could hang up on her. She had to admit she didn't particularly like it and decided it was time to do something about it. So she sent him a text. **Stop hanging up on me.**

When she didn't get an answer she sent another. **Please.**

This time, she got a reply right away.

Don't like it, do you?

No. I don't.

Another quick reply from Mack. **Neither do I.**

She groaned. **Fine. I'll only hang up on you when I really mean it.**

And, with that, she tossed down her phone and grinned. She didn't know what she wanted to do now, but there had to be something. She was willing to eat up the rest of the pasta though. It was just that this sister mystery was burning away at Doreen, and she wanted that snippy woman to call her back. How else could she find out? She walked outside and studied her neighbor's fence. He'd lived here for a while; maybe he knew. She walked over to the fence and called out, "Hello?"

There was a grump on the other side.

"I just wondered if you knew any of the Abelman family around here." She heard something being placed against the fence, and then Richard's face popped up over the top to look down at her.

"Wilma Abelman?" he asked.

"I'm not sure," she said. "That's possible though."

"There's Mickey Abelman. And Wilma is one of her daughters. They had four daughters. Mickey is the wife."

"*Hmm*, any more details?"

"Abelman, Abelman. Oh, wait, it was Gorenstein, Wilma Gorenstein."

"I'm looking for the sister of Reginald Abelman who had Johnson and Abelman Jewelers way back when."

Richard stared at her, his eyebrows slowly rising. "Are you looking into that old theft?" he asked, looking delighted.

"Maybe," she said cautiously, not understanding why he cared.

"A lot of us back then wanted to see that kid kicked out of the family," he said. "Now the old couple, they were really something. They were good people, but that son-in-law of theirs, he was a loser."

"Right," she said, sighing. "And what about their daughter?"

He just rolled his eyes at that. "Aretha has always been a snob," he said. "Born a snob, raised a snob, and carried on as a snob."

"Doesn't seem like anybody likes her," Doreen said thoughtfully.

"Nope. She doesn't like other people, and she makes it an obvious fact. So you immediately know where you stand with her. Except that you clearly don't stand on the same level."

Doreen nodded, hating to hear that because, of course, she'd seen so many people who were just the same. "Apparently not all the jewels were found, right?" Doreen said.

"No. There were rumors about some of the jewels showing up, but the cops couldn't identify them."

"Right, because the paperwork was supposedly destroyed in the fire."

"Well, that and Reginald couldn't produce the paperwork they needed for the insurance either," Richard said. "Like I said, that guy was a loser."

"It sure sounds like he was a mess," she said. "Maybe he did end up committing suicide."

"If that's what you call it," he said. "*Drug overdose.* ... When you think about it, suicide is a pretty demeaning slam. Means he wanted to get the hell away from her." At that, he snickered.

"Maybe," Doreen said, hating the need to defend Aretha. "But she was separated from him at the time."

"*Hmm.* I don't think the paperwork was finalized then," he said. "Still, it wasn't all that common to have a divorce back then. It still takes time to get the paperwork done."

"You think he might have committed suicide because of the divorce?" She hadn't considered that. Maybe he really did love Aretha. Maybe she was the one who saw him as a step up.

"If you ask me, you ought to take another look at that Aretha," he said. "If ever anybody deserved to be involved in a crime, it's her."

"She's really got your dander up, huh?"

"I walked into that store when she was just a young girl, but she was already snooty," he said. "I've seen her around town a couple times over the years, and my opinion hasn't changed."

"Interesting. Did you ever hear any rumors or theories about what might have happened to the jewels?"

He shrugged. "Probably went out of here through the pawn shop or maybe down to Vancouver. Or maybe there never were any. Maybe it was all forged paperwork, just to get the insurance company to pay out."

"They didn't pay out though," Doreen said. "The fire finished off everything that was left. The Johnsons depleted all the assets they had personally, trying to honor their debts and to pay what they could. Bankruptcy was inevitable then."

"And then they died," Richard said. "I remember it all was just like a never-ending stream of bad events. And Aretha ended up being the only one left standing." He looked at Doreen again with an eagle eye and said, "Remember that." Then he hopped back down again.

She frowned. "Do you know if Aretha had a sister-in-law?"

"I don't remember anything about one," he said.

She sagged, then nudged his memory. "One of the newspapers mentioned that Reginald Abelman had a sister. And his parents were from Vancouver."

"You could check the Vancouver phone book then," he said. "Did you think of that?"

She stopped and whispered, "No, I didn't."

She bolted back into the house and brought up the Vancouver white pages. She wasn't sure if she had free access to it. Soon enough she found it pretty easy to find the Abelmans of Vancouver. Hundreds of them. The trouble was, Abelman was a proper Jewish name.

She frowned at the long list. Then she ended up on one of those searches, finding an Abelman family tree. She thought that was fascinating. And there was Reginald's name, but it didn't say anything about other family members. She went back to the Abelman telephone listings. She went through and read them all, but they didn't mean anything, since it could be any one of them. And the woman on the phone had been correct in that, if the sister had married, it could be anybody else's number too, as the surname might have changed.

She went back to the family tree and took more time to study it. She frowned when she ran across another name she hadn't heard about before. *Norm.* She went back to the telephone listings and found a Norm Abelman. Immediately she phoned the number. When a gruff male answered, she asked if it was Norm.

"Yes. Who's calling?"

"I'm Doreen from Kelowna," she said.

"Yes, what do you want?" he asked.

"I'm looking for family members of a Reginald Abelman who lived in Kelowna," she said. "He died about thirty-seven years ago."

"Huh," the man said, but he didn't add anything else.

"Do you happen to know if he was part of your family? He married an Aretha Johnson," she said.

"Oh, right," he said. "His parents died."

"Yes, but were you related to his parents?"

"Cousins," he said. "The parents lived in Vancouver and died twenty-odd years ago. He headed off to Kelowna for better pastures not long after he hit his twenties and ended up marrying into a jewelry company or some such thing. I always thought he had the gall of a salesman to land that kind of an occupation."

"That's the one I was talking about," Doreen said, her excitement building inside.

"So, what about him?"

"I'm trying to find his sister," she said. She held her breath while she waited for him. She could almost feel the rusted old wheels turning in his mind as he tried to dredge up information.

"There was a sister," he said.

She frowned. "*Was* a sister? Does that mean she's dead?"

"You know what? I'm struggling to remember," he said. "But, yes, she's dead. I'm sure of it. But her daughter is not."

"Okay," Doreen said. "Do you know who her daughter is?"

"Well, you should know that," he said. "She lives in Kelowna."

"Wow," Doreen said. "I was hoping she lived here, but I don't have her last name. Or her first, for that matter."

Chapter 26

Wednesday Noon …

DOREEN TOOK A deep breath, trying to calm her frustration. It was one thing to talk to one person who didn't get you. It was another thing to talk to several who didn't get you. Because that usually meant Doreen was the problem. But she didn't think so in this case. "I can't find her under her maiden name," she said. "And I presume she married at some point."

"Oh, yes, she did. She moved up there after her brother separated from his wife. He needed a hand, and she was the older sister and always helped him out."

"Okay," she said. "Older sister?"

"No. No, I think I'm wrong there. I think she was younger." He shook his head. "No, she was older," he said, correcting himself. "She went up there and stayed for a while. Then she came back to Vancouver, got married here at some point, I believe, and had her daughter. And her daughter went back up to Kelowna. Yeah. I think that's how it went."

"Do you have his sister's name?"

"It was something funny," he said. "Like Lana or Lena.

It was weird."

"Okay, what about her daughter?"

He gave a bark of laughter at that. "You're damn lucky I'm remembering any of this," he said. "Most of the time I can't remember what I had for breakfast."

"If you could help me with a daughter's name, I'd really appreciate it," she said.

"I don't think I can remember that much. I'm trying. But I couldn't even get her mother's name."

"Right," Doreen said. "Is there anybody else in your family who would know?" she asked, trying hard to keep the note of worry out of her voice. She was desperate to find this name because it was important, but she didn't know how to contact anybody who would know.

"Well, maybe my daughter," he said. "She's the one working on the family tree."

"May I call her?"

"I don't know about that," he said, his voice turning cagey. "I'd better talk to her first. I'll call you back." And, with that, he hung up.

Doreen groaned. "You can only call me back if you saved my phone number somehow," she said.

And now she was frustrated again. The only way to deal with that was to go back outside and see if she could do something to get ready for the deck project. Or at least work in the garden. She had tons more to do there, never any question about that.

Looking at the lawn, she wondered again what it would cost to get in a bunch of large stones, or at least some crushed rock or something for a pathway. It was a long stretch, at least fifty feet to the creek. That would probably cost her a bundle. So it wouldn't happen right now, but she still needed to get a couple inches cleared right up against the fences. It would extend the life of the fence boards. Something to stop the garden from catching moisture and holding on to it next to the wooden fence.

She went to the end by the creek and started pulling the dirt away from the fence, cutting a clean border so she could keep the garden off the wood as she went. She soon sweated heavily.

Going back inside, she grabbed some water and forgot she had turned down her phone volume. She frowned when she saw a missed call. Groaning to herself, she hit the message and listened. Nothing was there, so she dialed the number back. And, sure enough, it was the old gentleman she'd talked to.

"She says you can call her," he said.

Delighted, Doreen walked to her notepad, grabbed the pen, and said, "What is her number?"

He read off the number and said, "Her name is Jennifer."

When he abruptly hung up, Doreen laughed out loud.

"How come so many people out there can't be socially friendly for longer than two minutes?" But it didn't matter now because she had a name and another number to try.

As soon as she dialed, a woman answered. "Hi, my name is Doreen."

"Oh, my gosh," the woman said. "My father called me about you. I'm Jennifer."

"Hi, Jennifer. I was just trying to find the name of the family members of Reginald Abelman who lived in Kelowna."

"Well, you know he married Aretha," Jennifer said, "and they filed for divorce, but the paperwork wasn't finalized when he overdosed." Her voice dropped in a mock despairing note. "The poor man, he must have been absolutely lovestruck."

"I'm sure that was it," Doreen said. *Not.* She didn't believe that theory for a second.

"It's all so terrible," she said.

"Do you know what his sister's name was?"

"I think I have it written down here somewhere," she said. "Oh, there it is. Lena," she said. "It's Lena."

"Good," Doreen said. "Did she marry?"

"She did, but then …" her voice trailed off. "You know, I have so many notes here. I keep trying to get organized, but I never quite make it."

"I can sympathize," Doreen said. "I've just done a massive clean-out of my place."

"Right. Still, I should have the information here somewhere."

"I guess the question is whether she's still married or not. It's her daughter I'm trying to find."

"The daughter. Yes, she had a daughter very young in life. I think she had her before she was married. There was a bit of a scandal about it, as I recall."

"Okay," Doreen said. "So do you know the name of the daughter?"

"You know what? I'm still looking for those notes." Her voice was distracted, and Doreen could hear a ton of paperwork being shuffled. She groaned. "I'm sorry. I'm so sorry," Jennifer said. "I'll have to call you back with it. I'll make it as soon as I can."

"That's fine," Doreen said. "I guess it's waited this long, so a little longer won't matter."

Jennifer sounded relieved. "I promise I have the information somewhere."

Undisturbed, Doreen said, "Okay, I look forward to hearing from you," and she hung up.

Now she had three people she was dealing with. She wrote down some notes, along with Jennifer's information and what little bit they had come up with and knew the easiest solution would be to talk to Aretha. But she didn't have her phone number. Looking down at the animals, she took a deep breath, remembering the last time.

"Road trip?" They all started going crazy. She picked up the leash and headed down the walking path toward Aretha's house. As she got closer, she could see the gates were locked. She pushed the Call button, but nobody answered. She sighed, then ripped off a clean page from her notepad. She addressed her note to Aretha, asking her to *Call Doreen*, jotting down her number. She tucked it into the mailbox, leaving a little bit of it sticking out, so they would see it.

She slowly headed past the house, determined to get enough of a walk in that she'd be tired by the time she got home. By now she was just boiling over with nervous energy. It was Wednesday, and the week was going by very quickly. All these people had been calling her back, yet she hadn't gotten any of the answers she wanted and needed. How frustrating.

Still, it was interesting to go back so many years and to hear everybody's interpretations of what had happened. She turned around to head back when she saw a vehicle pulling up to the driveway, but it was too far ahead for her to call out and get their attention. Somebody did stop and pick up her note from the mailbox. Smiling, she said, "Now call me, please."

Mugs just looked up at her. Thaddeus leaned against

her, as if to give her comfort, compassion, and support. She chuckled. "You guys are great," she said. "I don't know what I would have done without you all these months." As she continued her walk, her phone rang. She halted several houses away and looked at the screen. It was her. "Hi, Aretha," she said cheerfully.

"Why do you want me to call you?" Aretha asked. There was no panic, nothing in her voice other than curiosity.

"Honestly," Doreen said, "I'm trying to look into that burglary, and I was wondering if you could tell me your sister-in-law's name."

"Why?" she asked.

"It's just a puzzle piece I don't have."

"It was Lena or something," she said crossly. "I don't know why any of it matters."

"Right," Doreen said. "It was Lena. Though I just realized what I meant to ask you was about Lena's daughter. What was her name?"

"Oh, I don't remember," Aretha said. "She was an unwed mother, you know. I can't remember the details."

Doreen stared up at the sky. Was nobody else as curious as she was? "Okay. That's why I was trying to get a hold of you."

"It happened such a long time ago," Aretha said. "There isn't really anything you can do about it now."

"No," Doreen said, but, unable to resist, she added, "Except for the fact that not all the jewels were recovered."

"I know. I'm pretty sure my husband arranged for the theft, only that blew up too," she said. "He was trying to collect the insurance, I think, and then also keep a portion of the jewels. I spoke to my second husband about it several times, and that's what he assumed too."

"Which would have been tough because he was working for the insurance company that insured your business."

"Tell me about it," Aretha said with a groan. "We had a lot of discussions about it, but he wasn't mad at me."

"No," Doreen said. "That wouldn't have made any sense."

"No. Not at all." Aretha went on, "Now, if you're done with it, I'd like to go in and have a cup of tea."

"Of course, thank you very much." Then Doreen hung up.

She walked up the block. As she got closer to Aretha's house, a woman stepped out of the main gate in front of her. It was Heidi. Uncertain as to how the animals would act, Doreen cast a wary eye at Goliath. She tucked Mugs up closer and smiled gaily at Heidi. "Hi there. How are you doing?"

"Well, I'd be doing a lot better if you'd leave Aretha alone," she said.

Chapter 27

Wednesday Midafternoon …

"OH," DOREEN SAID. "Did she tell you that she just called me?"

"Yes, and about what?" she said, shaking her head. "That all happened so long ago."

"You're right," Doreen said. "But, when you think about it, some things were never solved."

"I know. I know," she said. "Something about jewels still missing."

"Exactly. I'm not sure who would be allowed ownership of them at this point," Doreen said, "but obviously Aretha could use the money."

At that, Heidi snorted. "I highly doubt anyone would hand them over to her."

"Maybe she still has some of them," Doreen said. "Did you ever think about that?"

"I did, indeed," Heidi said, laughing. "It was in the back of my mind that maybe she did have the jewels with her. But she's lived in my house for well over a year, and I can tell you that I've never seen any of them. I haven't seen any sign of her having any wealth beyond her decade-old clothes."

"Right," Doreen said, her heart sinking. She groaned. "That would be too much to hope for, wouldn't it?"

"If she had them, she would have sold them," Heidi said with conviction.

As they got closer, Mugs growled. Doreen looked down at him and frowned. "Mugs, behave yourself."

"Sorry about the other night," Heidi said. "I was a little disgruntled at something else happening in my day. I didn't mean to be snarky about the animals."

"You had every right to be," Doreen said. "Of course you don't want animals in your garden, and your garden is absolutely beautiful."

"Maybe," she said, as she looked around at the property. "This was one of Aretha's first husband's favorite properties. He used to spend a lot of time here." She smiled a mysterious smile.

"Was it his?" she asked in surprise.

"No," Heidi said. "It never was. But I know he was here a lot."

"Did you ever meet him?"

She shook her head. "Not really," and there was that mysterious smile.

"Does Aretha know that you know something about her ex-husband?"

"I don't think Aretha is living in this world very much nowadays." Heidi laughed. "She's at least twenty years my senior, and it's hard to see what I could possibly end up like," she admitted. "Aretha's memory is definitely going. She's got joint pain, and her stomach can't handle a lot of foods now."

"I guess that's to be expected to a certain extent," Doreen said cautiously. "But that's an interesting point. The stomach upsets could be from too much stress, worrying about her future. Maybe worrying about the jewel theft." She added the last as a stab in the dark.

"About what?" Heidi asked, looking at her. "That, if she'd had them, she would have sold them?"

"Of course she would have," Doreen said. "After hearing the story, I thought her first husband Reginald might have had something to do with it all."

"Why is that?"

"Because, after her parents died and then her husband Reginald died, the court cases fell into disarray."

"The court cases were all pending, but, after Reginald died, then there was nobody left to take to court," she said with a laugh. Heidi raised a glance and gave Doreen a superior smile. "You with all your puzzle-solving abilities didn't consider that? Surely you didn't believe Aretha and her suicide version, did you? Of course, it makes her feel better to believe he did it out of remorse."

"I'm trying to get a copy of the death certificate," Doreen said. "Just to make sure it was suicide."

"That won't help," she said, "because it could say overdose, but that wouldn't mean he overdosed himself. Now he might have, but who are we to know what really happened?"

"True enough," Doreen said, but for some reason she felt a little uneasy. And Mugs wasn't cooperating. Goliath was, however. He sat right at her feet. However, Heidi kept smiling, but the smile was a little bit disconcerting too. She looked down at Goliath. "I should get the animals home."

"You do that," Heidi said with another unsettling smile. "And, if you find any jewels, let me know."

"Hah! Wouldn't that be nice?" she said.

"According to the grapevine, you found some."

At that, Doreen turned and looked at her. "And who told you that?" she asked.

Heidi shrugged. "It's the local gossip." Her gaze narrowed. "Did you?"

"If I did," she said, "I certainly wouldn't be passing that news around."

"Of course not," Heidi said. "You wouldn't want anybody to break in, would you?"

"I've had several break-ins lately," Doreen said, her nose inching up slightly. "The last thing I'd want is more." And with a wave of goodbye, she turned and hurried away. She knew in her heart she wouldn't be dealing with Heidi anymore. This version was the complete opposite of the fun-loving gardener she'd met the first couple times. Feeling like Heidi's gaze glared into the back of her head, she resisted the urge to turn around and look because she knew instinctively Heidi *was* watching. When she got home, she phoned Mack.

His voice was distracted. "Now what?"

"It's Heidi," she said. "Something's very off about her," and Doreen related the conversation.

"That's not good," he said. "Don't you have a safety deposit box someplace where you can keep the gems?"

"No," Doreen said, "and I highly suspect that's why your mom never did anything with them either. She didn't want to get any undue attention because of it."

"No," he said. "That makes sense."

"Did you ever see Reginald's death certificate?"

"I did," he said. "He overdosed. His death certificate says *accidental overdose*."

"Interesting."

"Why?

"What kind of poison?" she asked.

"Well, let's put it this way. It was an overdose. *Accidental* overdose. A mixture of all kinds of drugs in it. As if he tossed it all into his drink and drank it up."

"Interesting."

"You keep saying that," he said in exasperation. "That doesn't mean it was murder."

"What if he didn't want a divorce, and what if it was murder?" she asked.

"Are you suspecting Aretha?"

"I don't know what I'm suspecting," Doreen said with a heavy groan. "This case has got me befuddled."

"Good," he said, "now you know how we feel."

She laughed. "I am a little worried now though, after Heidi's comment about the rumor saying I have the jewels and someone breaking in."

"You should be," he said. "Make sure you set that security system."

"Right," she said. "And, if I send you a weird text, take it as a warning sign and come, would you?"

There was silence on the other end. "Are you thinking you're seriously in danger?" His voice sounded brusque.

"Yeah," she said. "It feels like something really weird is going on."

"What? *Something really weird is going on* and you feeling you're in danger aren't the same thing."

"I know," she said. However, as soon as she hung up, she put on a cup of tea to make herself feel better.

About an hour later—after she'd vacuumed the house, scrubbed both bathrooms, and done laundry—she realized she was filling her mind by keeping her hands busy, trying to stop thinking about everything going on. When a knock came on her door, she checked the window first. There stood

Aretha. She opened her door. "Hi," Doreen said.

"I was thinking about what you were saying," Aretha said.

"Do you want to come in and talk?"

Aretha stepped in and looked around. "You don't have much furniture."

"No," Doreen said. "I cleaned it all out, and now I'm slowly building up a few pieces." She motioned to the two pot chairs. Aretha sat down, her legs tucked under in a ladylike way. Doreen sat down and crossed her legs, the opposite of what her husband would have wanted. "Now," she said. "What is it you wanted to tell me?"

"Well, the thing is, I couldn't tell you at the time, but Heidi is my niece. She didn't want anyone to know because of all the mess in my history."

Doreen stared at her in shock.

Aretha nodded. "She's the loveliest woman, and obviously I didn't want to room with somebody who wasn't family."

"Of course," Doreen said. "I wish you would have told me that originally. Then I wouldn't have spent days trying to track down the name."

"It was out of respect for Heidi that I didn't, as she asked me not to. And, of course, she's done much better than I ever have," she said sadly. "I did everything I could to make things better, but I could do only so much."

Chapter 28

Wednesday Late Afternoon …

"HAVE YOU EVER seen any of the jewels?" Doreen asked Aretha.

"I saw something I thought were jewels in Reginald's hand once, but, when I asked, he just laughed and said it was nothing. I always wondered if he'd found some while cleaning up after the break-in and didn't put them back into the store's inventory. I didn't want to believe it, but he was bitter, often saying he'd lost everything. Of course he had. But so had I," Aretha whispered.

"What about your new husband? Didn't he want those jewels to combat the insurance claims?"

She lifted her hands. "What would I tell him? It was years later, and I didn't know what had happened to them for sure, and Reginald was dead. It was all such a nightmare, and I just wanted to forget."

"You said Reginald left you a note, saying more jewels were hidden in the city."

"Yes, but he never told me where."

"Do you have any idea what kind of a place he would have chosen?"

"Only that he always made bad decisions, so, no matter where it was, it's probably long gone."

"Did Heidi know?"

"We've never spoken about it," she said.

Doreen hesitated, not sure if she should tell her. "She told me that she'd never seen you wearing any."

"Of course not," Aretha said. "I hate to say it, but I've been forced to sell everything. And even now I barely have enough to pay Heidi."

"But Heidi's done very well?"

"She's done very well," she said. "She once told me that she got a surprise inheritance from her mother."

"Interesting," she said.

Aretha looked at her and frowned. "In what way?"

Doreen smiled and shrugged. "An awful lot of dead people are involved in this scenario."

"True," Aretha said. "Sometimes I wish I was one of them. Growing old gracefully is one thing. Growing old and broke and graceful is a whole different problem," she said with half a smile.

"True enough," Doreen said, understanding more than Aretha knew. "And you trust Heidi, correct?"

Aretha nodded. "Yes. Of course I do. Why?"

"I just wondered if she thought maybe you would leave her the jewels when you passed on."

"I don't have anything to leave her," Aretha said sadly. "Even my second husband didn't leave me enough to live on. I knew he was lost and still in love with his first wife, but I was looking for companionship, so I took what was offered. But I think I shortchanged myself both times."

"So how did you end up moving in with Heidi?" Doreen asked.

"She offered," Aretha said. "She came to me one day, and we were talking. I told her how upset I was about the way my life had worked out. All of it, starting with never having the burglary solved."

"Did Heidi's mother suspect her brother?"

Aretha nodded. "Her mother had said something about it to her." She looked thoughtful. "Everyone with answers is dead."

"So very true."

"It *is* true, and it's very insensitive of you to be digging into this," Heidi said, suddenly walking through the kitchen into the living room. Mugs jumped to his feet. She looked down at him and sneered. "What kind of watchdog are you? I came in through the open kitchen door without you even knowing."

Aretha looked at her in surprise. "Why didn't you come with me?" she asked. "And why didn't you tell me that you were coming here?"

"I came to hear if there was any conversation to help us find those jewels," Heidi said. "Because you realize Doreen has found some."

Aretha looked at Heidi in shock and then turned her gaze to Doreen. "Is that true?"

"Heidi seems to have heard some rumors in town," Doreen said. She had her phone in her hand and looked down at it, then smiled and swiped to the right, as if checking for email or something, and brought up Mack's text. She looked up at Heidi and said, "But rumors are just that, rumors."

"Do you think the jewels are still here in town?" Aretha leaned forward and placed her hand on Doreen's knee. "Is it possible?"

Doreen looked at her gently. "What difference would it make if they were?"

"Well, they would belong to me," she said, hope in her gaze. "The insurance company never paid on the claim for coverage, and the files have been closed. It would make a huge difference in my life if any jewels were found."

"How much of a difference did it make in the beginning?" Doreen asked. "Did you have anything to do with the death of your husband?"

Tears came to Aretha's eyes. "No. He was a screwup, and I knew that. But I loved him. And just like I was saying about my second husband loving his first wife, my heart died with my first. I wanted the divorce because I couldn't live with him and all his chaos, but I didn't want to let him go," she whispered.

"And what about you, Heidi?" Doreen asked. "Did you ever wonder how your uncle died?"

"He overdosed on drugs," she said. "I'm sure it was a suicide. I told you that."

"Maybe," Doreen said. "But what did his sister, your mother, die of?"

"Cancer."

"And what do you want to bet the same drugs his sister was on are what killed your husband?" Doreen asked Aretha.

Aretha shook her head. "So he went for a visit and took all her drugs. That just makes her a victim too."

A glance at Heidi revealed her glaring at Doreen. "But Heidi knows the truth. Don't you, Heidi?"

"So my mother's drugs were used. Big deal," she said. "Do you have any idea how many people die from drug overdoses every day?"

But the question hadn't fazed Heidi. "Did you kill your

mother?" Doreen asked Heidi out of the blue.

Heidi shook her head. "The cancer took her."

"And then you found her diaries, I presume?"

"Actually she told me on her deathbed, but I was too young. I didn't really understand everything. But I taped it all and wrote it down, determined to come and look for it when I could."

"Look for what?" Aretha asked. "Are you saying my husband was murdered?"

Heidi nodded. "My mother killed him. She knew about the jewels he had kept from the insurance fraud. He stole the jewels and hoped to get the insurance payout too. But he wasn't the brightest light on the string."

Aretha cried out again, her hand going to her mouth. "So he *did* cause all that? I wondered but had hoped not …"

"My mother was involved in the break-in too," Heidi said. "She came up one night and helped him out, then disappeared with a bunch of the jewels afterward. But she made some bad decisions herself and couldn't get much for the jewels. Uncle Reginald had a bunch he hid around the city. You're right, Aretha. He was a screwup. And he left Lena notes about where they all were. She found one pile, and that kept her going for her cancer treatments, and she gave me some. That's how I managed to buy the big estate I've got. And, of course, through my marriage we lived here, but when Jorgensen died, it was already paid off because I'd made sure it was."

"Did your husband know of your ill-gotten gains?" Doreen asked.

Heidi shrugged. "No. He didn't ask too many questions. It's not like I wanted anybody in my life who would be smarter than me."

"Of course not," Doreen said softly. "And what about the last bag of jewels?"

"They were gone," she said. "The bag with the big emerald was gone. That's the one we've been looking for. I figured, when Aretha died, I'd go through all her stuff better and find it. But I haven't seen anything of it yet."

"You've been through my things?" Aretha asked.

"Of course. Isn't that the reason you moved into the house too?" Heidi asked cynically. "To see if I had any of them?"

"It crossed my mind that maybe you did," Aretha said, "because you seemed to have done so well for yourself."

"I did. I had quite a few of them, and you're right, I did do well for myself. But I didn't kill anybody," Heidi said. "Although Doreen might be my first."

"What? If I don't hand over the jewels, you'll kill me?"

"Of course," Heidi said. "Because I'm running out of money and I have no intention of being poor, like Aretha."

"You can always sell your house," Doreen said drily.

"Not happening," she said. "When you're accustomed to a certain lifestyle, you'll do anything to maintain it."

"I don't think so," Doreen said, standing up. "I don't have any jewels, ladies, so you'll have to excuse me. I'm feeling tired. I think a nap may be in order."

"I don't think so," Heidi said, and, within an instant, she had a gun in her hand.

Doreen looked at it and sighed. "You know what? I'm really tired of getting knocked around, beaten up, and shot at," she said.

Aretha stood and whispered, "Heidi, what are you doing?"

"What I should have done when I first heard about

them, and that was a couple days ago." She motioned the gun at Doreen. "Go get them."

Doreen shook her head. "I don't know what you're talking about."

Heidi stepped closer, into the living room, and it was all Doreen could do to keep the smile off her face as she watched Goliath slink under the pot chairs, going in behind Heidi. Doreen knew what would happen next, even if Heidi didn't. Thaddeus had been on the kitchen table, but he suddenly appeared on the round newel post of the staircase.

Heidi looked at him in disgust. "All these animals," she said. "They're just nasty."

Thaddeus started to sing, "Thaddeus is gorgeous."

Heidi looked at him. "He's not for real, is he?"

"Oh, yeah, he is," Doreen said with a sigh. "What are you doing with that gun? Either shoot me, and then, of course, shoot Aretha as well, or put it away and forget about the jewels."

"That's not happening," Heidi said. She cocked the gun and pointed it at Doreen.

"So you'll kill your aunt too?"

"She won't say anything," Heidi said. "Otherwise she'll end up in some government-run old-age home with nothing to redeem her lifestyle."

Aretha's eyes widened, and she looked from one to the other.

Doreen worried it just might be possible, and she didn't want to put it to the test.

Just then, Thaddeus asked, "Are you done?"

Heidi spun around and glared at him. Taking advantage of the distraction, Doreen stepped forward and tried to wrench the gun free. But Heidi turned it back on her and pressed it hard against her shoulder. "Back off," Heidi said.

Thaddeus hopped onto her shoulder and dug his claws in.

The only problem with that was, it was the arm holding the gun. And Heidi's trigger finger would flex in response to a claw to that shoulder. Doreen managed to knock her arm to the side, just as Thaddeus dug in hard.

Heidi shrieked and shot off the gun, a bullet slamming into the wall above the door.

Doreen tried to grab her hand, but Heidi was strong and fit.

Mugs jumped up in front of her, and Goliath had apparently chosen the back of Heidi for his target this time. He stretched up and caught her in the back of the knees with his claws.

Heidi buckled and landed on her knees; then Mugs sent her flying backward yet again.

With that accomplished, Doreen managed to pull the gun free and held it on Heidi.

In the background, she could hear vehicles tearing up the cul-de-sac into the driveway.

"You guys are awesome," she said warmly to her furry and feathered family. "And it sounds like the cavalry has arrived."

The door opened, and Mack stepped in. When he saw Doreen with a gun on Heidi, he groaned. "Couldn't you have just gotten out of trouble instead of into trouble just this one time?"

Doreen smiled and said, "How about next time?" Then she handed him the gun. "We have here a classic case of Heidi's mother having killed her brother, Reginald Abelman, and Heidi was only helping out Aretha to find the missing jewels herself."

"The jewels that my mother found?" Mack asked for clarity.

Doreen nodded. "Absolutely. Those jewels. And we already have a buyer, if we can ever figure out who the heck is the rightful owner." She looked at Aretha, who sat there, her hand clasped over her mouth, with tears in her eyes as she stared at her niece.

"I suspect it might be Aretha," Doreen muttered to Mack, "but I'm not sure."

He looked from one to the other, then shook his head. "It's not your problem now," he said.

She turned to see Chester and Arnold and grinned. "Hi, guys."

"What kind of trouble are you in now?" Chester muttered.

"I just solved the burglary from a long time ago and a murder too," she said. "But unfortunately nobody's left to prosecute."

"Why is that?" Chester asked, narrowing his gaze.

"Because Heidi's mother killed her brother, which is currently an accidental overdose on your books," she said. "And the two of them were involved in the burglary and the insurance fraud attempt by the jewelry store."

"And my uncle also burned the business to the ground," Heidi spat from her position on the ground.

"Interesting," Doreen said. "Did they have anything to do with the death of Aretha's parents?"

"My mother said she cut the brake lines," Heidi said, as the men pulled her to her feet.

Aretha gasped, her hands dropping from her face to her heart.

"Wow," Chester said. "All from so long ago."

"Yep," Doreen said. "But just think, guys. No bodies this time. Just paperwork."

At that, Chester groaned. "Paperwork? More paperwork?"

"More paperwork," she said with a big chuckle. "But that's all right. You guys are up for it."

"If you say so," Arnold snapped. "Any chance you could just stay out of trouble for once?"

Doreen made a dusting off motion with her hands and said, "Absolutely. You take this lovely lady out of my life, and I'll be more than happy to."

"But do we have anything to charge her with?"

"Aside from trying to shoot me just now? That bullet hole she put in my wall is proof. Also I highly suggest you look into her husband's death," Doreen said. "She's a little too happy he's gone."

Heidi glared at her. "You don't know anything about it."

"No, I don't," she said, "but I'm sure the police will get to the bottom of it."

Mack just smiled, and, before Doreen knew it, Heidi was handcuffed and stood on her feet. She looked back at Doreen. "You're just nothing but an interfering busybody."

"And you're selfish and greedy and conniving. You only moved here to find all those jewels, and you manipulated your aunt into your house, just so you could keep an eye on her, in case more jewels were found."

"She needed a place to live."

"She still needs a place to live," Doreen said with a smile. "You'll let her live there while you're in jail?"

"I'm not going to jail for anything more than a misdemeanor. I'll be out in no time," Heidi said.

"Until they dig up your husband's body and take another look at that. How did he die?"

Heidi glared at her. "None of your business."

But Doreen answered for her. "He committed suicide, right?" she said. "He ingested a whole pile of antibiotics and other medications."

"Oh, my God. How did you get him to take them?" Aretha asked.

Heidi didn't answer.

Yet Doreen looked at her and knew. "The same way her mom got your uncle to take his medication," she said. "She pointed a gun at him and insisted." She glared at Heidi. "Right?"

Heidi stiffened her back. "None of your business."

But everybody nodded.

"Exactly," Chester said. "Wow. You could have just shot him. It would have been easier."

"Not necessarily. It would have left a lot more forensic evidence," Heidi snapped.

"So," Doreen said, "now that you'll be in prison for murdering your husband, does Aretha get to stay at the house?"

Heidi's shoulders sagged. "I'll think about it."

Doreen turned to Aretha, who stared at her niece with a hopeful expression. "You might as well put her out of her misery now. She needs a place to live."

"She's already there, isn't she?" Heidi said. "At least for the moment she can stay."

Aretha's face burst into a big smile. "I'll look after it," she promised.

"Somebody needs to. We'll figure it out," Heidi grumped.

Aretha reached out to grasp Doreen's hands and whispered, "Thank you."

"You're welcome. And, if you take care of paying the bills and everything else," she said, "I think you are due a stipend for looking after the property."

Heidi stopped and called out, "Enough of that talk."

"No, I don't think so," Doreen continued. "Aretha will have to bring in gardeners now that you won't be there. She'll have to pay the bills and handle all kinds of things. I think she needs at least one thousand a month in order to take care of that."

Heidi just glared at her, then turned to look to her aunt and sighed. "I'll see," she said. "No promises."

Aretha grasped Doreen's fingers and whispered, "Thank you. Thank you. Thank you."

As she started to go down the front steps, Heidi turned. "What about the jewels?"

Mack shook his head. "I wouldn't think about them, if I were you." And he promptly ushered her toward Arnold and Chester.

"Oh, but—" Aretha tried to interject.

"I think Zachary deserves to finally get the emerald he wants for his beloved wife, and that money—plus the money from selling the other jewels—well, I think a charity might be the best answer," Doreen said gently. "We don't want anybody thinking you had anything to do with this in order to get those jewels, do we?" she asked Aretha.

Aretha's eyes lit up with horror. "No," she said. "If I can get one thousand a month from my niece to look after the place and be able to stay there ..." She smiled in delight. "You know what? Maybe after all this, a charity is the right answer." She looked down at the animals. "How about an animal charity? My vote is for giving all these guys as much care as they need. I'm really glad Heidi didn't manage to shoot you."

"Me too," Doreen said. She waved as Aretha started the walk home. Then she whispered to herself again, "Me too."

Epilogue

Wednesday Late Afternoon ...

ARNOLD AND CHESTER prepared to leave, each one of them holding onto one of Heidi's arms.

"That was a good thing you did," Mack said quietly.

She gave him a quiet smile. "Someone needed to help her. Now, of course, I don't have a case to work on ..." She looked at Mack hopefully. He stiffened and glared at her. "None of mine."

"Don't you have another case in progress?" Arnold asked.

"No," Doreen said with a big smile. "I figured I'd look into these old ladies dropping dead."

"You are the gardener," Chester said, with that fat smile of his. "If anybody can figure out what kiwis have to do with that damn case, I'd like to know."

Doreen stared at him. "Kiwis?"

Mack sent a warning look to Chester, but it was already too late. Chester was too far ahead.

"Yep," he said. "A kiwi in the mouth."

"But only one of the old women's mouths?"

He leaned forward and said in that thick heavy whisper,

"Yes, but all three had one on their person."

Doreen grinned. "*Killer in the Kiwis*. I love it." That was so her next case.

Mack shot her a hard look. "You stay out of it," he said. "Cold cases are one thing, but my cases are another."

She grinned up at him impudently. "No problem," she said. "You've got, let's see, what? Twenty-four hours?"

Mack jammed his hands on his hips, as Arnold started to chuckle. Whistling, he walked over to Chester and the two of them loaded Heidi into the back seat of their RCMP patrol car, leaving Doreen with Mack.

Doreen turned and looked up at him. "So?"

"So, what?" he growled.

"Twenty-four hours? Forty-eight? How much lead time do you need?" she asked hopefully. He took a hard step toward her, but she no longer felt threatened by Mack. She looked up at him and grinned. "Come on. Forty-eight hours it is then. It's a deal. I'm on the *Killer in the Kiwis* case."

Laughing, she raced into the kitchen. She heard the front door slam as Mack walked out, and she knew he had to leave. He now had even more work to do at the police station. And that was fine.

She'd give him the two days but not a minute more.

This concludes Book 10 of Lovely Lethal Gardens:
Jewels in the Juniper.
Read about Killer in the Kiwis:
Lovely Lethal Gardens, Book 11

Lovely Lethal Gardens: Killer in the Kiwis (Book #11)

A new cozy mystery series from *USA Today* best-selling author Dale Mayer. Follow gardener and amateur sleuth Doreen Montgomery—and her amusing and mostly lovable cat, dog, and parrot—as they catch murderers and solve crimes in lovely Kelowna, British Columbia.

Riches to rags. … Chaos again. … Winning is important, … at least for some!

Doreen is overwhelmed with joy when she sees all the volunteers who show up to help get her deck addition built. Most of the men are cops, friends of Corporal Mack Moreau's, and are happy to help Mack's special friend and the lady who has helped solve so many crimes for them with a spot of home renovation.

But before the deck improvement can be finished, duty calls, and the cops are called away on a case. *Another* gray-haired lady has dropped dead. Yet another heart attack victim is added to the long line of previous ones. And, of course, neither of these recently deceased women had a heart condition that would explain their sudden demise.

With her animals at her side, Doreen is determined to figure out what the ladies had in common, plus why and how kiwis keep popping up in this case. As she digs into the ladies' lives, the things Doreen discover are shocking, … but not as shocking as the answer is to this riddle …

Find Book 11 here!
To find out more visit Dale Mayer's website.
https://geni.us/DMKillerUniversal

Author's Note

Thank you for reading Jewels in the Juniper: Lovely Lethal Gardens, Book 10! If you enjoyed the book, please take a moment and leave a short review.

Dear reader,

I love to hear from readers, and you can contact me at my website: www.dalemayer.com or at my Facebook author page. To be informed of new releases and special offers, sign up for my newsletter or follow me on BookBub. And if you are interested in joining Dale Mayer's Reader Group, here is the Facebook sign up page.
http://geni.us/DaleMayerFBGroup

Cheers,
Dale Mayer

About the Author

Dale Mayer is a *USA Today* best-selling author, best known for her SEALs military romances, her Psychic Visions series, and her Lovely Lethal Garden cozy series. Her contemporary romances are raw and full of passion and emotion (Broken But ... Mending, Hathaway House series). Her thrillers will keep you guessing (Kate Morgan, By Death series), and her romantic comedies will keep you giggling (*It's a Dog's Life*, a stand-alone novella; and the Broken Protocols series, starring Charming Marvin, the cat).

Dale honors the stories that come to her—and some of them are crazy, break all the rules and cross multiple genres!

To go with her fiction, she also writes nonfiction in many different fields, with books available on résumé writing, companion gardening, and the US mortgage system. All her books are available in print and ebook format.

Connect with Dale Mayer Online

Dale's Website – www.dalemayer.com
Twitter – @DaleMayer
Facebook Page – geni.us/DaleMayerFBFanPage
Facebook Group – geni.us/DaleMayerFBGroup
BookBub – geni.us/DaleMayerBookbub
Instagram – geni.us/DaleMayerInstagram
Goodreads – geni.us/DaleMayerGoodreads
Newsletter – geni.us/DaleNews

Also by Dale Mayer

Published Adult Books:

Hathaway House

Aaron, Book 1

Brock, Book 2

Cole, Book 3

Denton, Book 4

Elliot, Book 5

Finn, Book 6

Gregory, Book 7

Heath, Book 8

Iain, Book 9

Jaden, Book 10

Keith, Book 11

The K9 Files

Ethan, Book 1

Pierce, Book 2

Zane, Book 3

Blaze, Book 4

Lucas, Book 5

Parker, Book 6

Carter, Book 7

Weston, Book 8

Greyson, Book 9

Psychic Visions Books 4–6
Psychic Visions Books 7–9

By Death Series
Touched by Death
Haunted by Death
Chilled by Death
By Death Books 1–3

Broken Protocols – Romantic Comedy Series
Cat's Meow
Cat's Pajamas
Cat's Cradle
Cat's Claus
Broken Protocols 1-4

Broken and... Mending
Skin
Scars
Scales (of Justice)
Broken but... Mending 1-3

Glory
Genesis
Tori
Celeste
Glory Trilogy

Biker Blues
Morgan: Biker Blues, Volume 1
Cash: Biker Blues, Volume 2

SEALs of Honor

Heroes for Hire

Levi's Legend: Heroes for Hire, Book 1
Stone's Surrender: Heroes for Hire, Book 2
Merk's Mistake: Heroes for Hire, Book 3
Rhodes's Reward: Heroes for Hire, Book 4
Flynn's Firecracker: Heroes for Hire, Book 5
Logan's Light: Heroes for Hire, Book 6
Harrison's Heart: Heroes for Hire, Book 7
Saul's Sweetheart: Heroes for Hire, Book 8
Dakota's Delight: Heroes for Hire, Book 9
Michael's Mercy (Part of Sleeper SEAL Series)
Tyson's Treasure: Heroes for Hire, Book 10
Jace's Jewel: Heroes for Hire, Book 11
Rory's Rose: Heroes for Hire, Book 12
Brandon's Bliss: Heroes for Hire, Book 13
Liam's Lily: Heroes for Hire, Book 14
North's Nikki: Heroes for Hire, Book 15
Anders's Angel: Heroes for Hire, Book 16
Reyes's Raina: Heroes for Hire, Book 17
Dezi's Diamond: Heroes for Hire, Book 18
Vince's Vixen: Heroes for Hire, Book 19
Ice's Icing: Heroes for Hire, Book 20
Johan's Joy: Heroes for Hire, Book 21
Galen's Gemma: Heroes for Hire, Book 22
Heroes for Hire, Books 1–3
Heroes for Hire, Books 4–6
Heroes for Hire, Books 7–9
Heroes for Hire, Books 10–12
Heroes for Hire, Books 13–15

SEALs of Steel

Badger: SEALs of Steel, Book 1

Erick: SEALs of Steel, Book 2
Cade: SEALs of Steel, Book 3
Talon: SEALs of Steel, Book 4
Laszlo: SEALs of Steel, Book 5
Geir: SEALs of Steel, Book 6
Jager: SEALs of Steel, Book 7
The Final Reveal: SEALs of Steel, Book 8
SEALs of Steel, Books 1–4
SEALs of Steel, Books 5–8
SEALs of Steel, Books 1–8

The Mavericks

Kerrick, Book 1
Griffin, Book 2
Jax, Book 3
Beau, Book 4
Asher, Book 5
Ryker, Book 6
Miles, Book 7
Nico, Book 8
Keane, Book 9
Lennox, Book 10
Gavin, Book 11
Shane, Book 12

Bullard's Battle Series

Ryland's Reach, Book 1
Cain's Cross, Book 2
Eton's Escape, Book 3
Garret's Gambit, Book 4
Kano's Keep, Book 5
Fallon's Flaw, Book 6

Quinn's Quest, Book 7
Bullard's Beauty, Book 8

Collections
Dare to Be You…
Dare to Love…
Dare to be Strong…
RomanceX3

Standalone Novellas
It's a Dog's Life
Riana's Revenge
Second Chances

Published Young Adult Books:

Family Blood Ties Series
Vampire in Denial
Vampire in Distress
Vampire in Design
Vampire in Deceit
Vampire in Defiance
Vampire in Conflict
Vampire in Chaos
Vampire in Crisis
Vampire in Control
Vampire in Charge
Family Blood Ties Set 1–3
Family Blood Ties Set 1–5
Family Blood Ties Set 4–6
Family Blood Ties Set 7–9
Sian's Solution, A Family Blood Ties Series Prequel

Novelette

Design series
Dangerous Designs
Deadly Designs
Darkest Designs
Design Series Trilogy

Standalone
In Cassie's Corner
Gem Stone (a Gemma Stone Mystery)
Time Thieves

Published Non-Fiction Books:

Career Essentials
Career Essentials: The Résumé
Career Essentials: The Cover Letter
Career Essentials: The Interview
Career Essentials: 3 in 1